THE THREE SISTERS TRILOGY BOOK 2

TANGLEWOOD MAGIC

USA TODAY BESTSELLING AUTHOR

GENEVIEVE JACK

Tanglewood Magic: The Three Sisters, Book 2

Copyright © Genevieve Jack 2021

Published by Carpe Luna Ltd, Bloomington, IL 61704

This book is a work of fiction. Names, characters, places, and incidents are either products of the author's imagination or used fictitiously. Any resemblance to actual events, locales, or persons, living or dead, is entirely coincidental.

All rights reserved. No part of this publication can be reproduced or transmitted in any form or by any means, electronic or mechanical, without permission in writing from the author or publisher.

First Edition: August 2021

eISBN: 978-1-940675-77-0

Paperback: 978-1-940675-78-7

1.2

About the Book

Her magical strength is transformation, but is she powerful enough to change his heart?

A witch in the crosshairs

Circe Tanglewood has tried to fit in with the other witches of Darnuith, but since the day her sister became queen, she's been the target of painful rumors and vicious threats. Aside from her sisters, her only friend is the owner of the apothecary where she works. Her heart wants more from the taciturn and commanding Rhys, but she's hesitant to risk losing her sole ally.

A wizard with a past

Rhys Bloodgood has suffered loss and never plans to open himself up to it again. No matter how attracted he is to Circe, allowing himself to love her is a gamble he's not ready to take. Besides, a failed relationship might lose him a talented apprentice.

A war that will either bring them together or tear them apart

Rhys and Circe must work together to save Queen Medea from a poisoning attempt, which shatters the walls between them and drives them into the mounting political turmoil between Darnuith and Paragon. When friends become lovers, there's nothing like the magical high, but the perils of finding Medea's would-be assassin could destroy them before they even have a chance to begin.

"Go back where you came from!" The hateful words traveled through the walls of the apothecary where Circe worked and hit her right in the heart.

Reflexively, she raised her wand and cast a defensive spell toward the front window, just as the assailant's blast shattered the glass. Fates' blessing, her magic successfully halted the explosion. She grunted with the effort of holding the window together, the tip of her wand glowing purple. But while she'd saved herself from a face full of glass, mending the spider-web crack proved problematic. If she lowered her wand for even a moment in order to throw the next spell, the shards would surely fall apart.

"*Synchónefsi!*" Rhys Bloodgood stormed from his laboratory, his wand flashing emerald before his spell plowed into the glass. The pieces fused themselves, brilliantly. Circe lowered her wand, relieved the window looked new again.

"Thank you," she offered, but Rhys wasn't listening.

Without even pausing his stride, he thrust through the front door, looking both ways for the vandal.

"They're long gone," Circe called. "Flew by on their broom faster than a falcon. It was a man, but I didn't get a good look. Had the hood of his cloak pulled over his face."

"Fates' fury." Rhys marched inside and slammed the door. Circe braced herself, hoping the reverberation wouldn't shatter the front window again. She was relieved when the glass held.

She sighed and shook her head. "Listen, Rhys..."

"Don't."

"You have to let me go. I'm not good for business." Circe certainly wouldn't blame him for firing her. Guilt plagued her over the position she'd put him in.

There was no question that the attack and the message that came with it were meant for her. Since her sister Medea had been named queen of Darnuith, the violence and threats against Circe and her sisters had gradually increased in intensity. Never mind that Medea had been magically chosen for the role by the Fates during the ritual of the Sacred Lots and named by her predecessor, Ferula Northstar, with her last breath. Never mind that Medea wouldn't have ever chosen the role for herself.

The people of Darnuith had thrust the title upon Medea and then immediately criticized her for taking it. All because Circe, Medea, and Isis Tanglewood had grown up in the Garden of the Hesperides. They had come to Darnuith as strangers. Medea's selection was highly unusual. Not only was it the first time a chosen queen hadn't been born on Darnuith soil, it was the first time the prior queen's adviser was not chosen for the role.

Zelaria, the previous queen's adviser, had trained at Ferula's side for decades and had offered sacrifices to the Fates. It was only natural for the people here to assume history would repeat itself. When Medea's stone glowed and Ferula whispered her name, the crowd initially acknowledged the results. Zelaria accepted Medea as queen and agreed to continue as her adviser.

But over time, Darnuith's outward agreement with the results became overshadowed by growing rumors the three sisters couldn't contain. People had barely trusted them before. It was too easy for the citizens of Darnuith to believe that their otherness was cause for concern. Perhaps the Sacred Lots didn't work with someone like them in the mix. Perhaps their magic altered the proper results. Suspicions about the validity of the selection had grown to a fever pitch recently and, with it, the violence.

Go back where you came from.

"You're not going anywhere," Rhys said firmly. "I won't let a few small-minded imbeciles bully me out of a trained employee."

"Rhys... It's not just a few. Business has dropped off this season. It's because of me. I don't feel right costing you income."

He leveled a dark stare on her that sent a shiver along her spine. Rhys Bloodgood did not suffer fools. The intensity of being the center of his attention made her knees weak. His mind was razor-sharp, and when he focused on her, she could feel it cut right through her like his surgeon's blade.

"I wish you to stay." His voice was eerily quiet. "Now, unless you plan to walk out on me, I need your assistance with something in my laboratory."

Without another word, he strode toward the back room from where he'd come, his command lingering in the air around her, expecting to be obeyed.

Circe released a deep, relieved breath and followed him. The truth was that if he'd told her to stand on her head, she would have obeyed—or tried to anyway. Rhys had that effect on her. There was something about his voice that made her want to please him. Plus, she was grateful he wanted her to stay. This job was her favorite thing about living in Darnuith. If Rhys still wanted her here, she wasn't going anywhere.

The attacks on her and her sisters were testing her in the most personal way. For most of her life, Circe Tanglewood had thought of herself as a conformist. While her sisters Medea and Isis acted as if every rule was meant to be broken, she preferred to keep her feet firmly on the ground and her steps safely on a well-worn path. Although she'd gone along with her sisters' risky schemes in the past, it was only after much cajoling and voicing her fears about their antics. It wasn't so much that she feared punishment or injury as she thought things simply worked better when there was order.

Now, she had people breaking windows to try to scare her from her job. Worse had happened at the home she shared with Isis. Dead animals left on their lawn. Ill wishes thrown through their windows. Neither of them had stepped a hair out of line to invite such behavior. In fact, Circe's accommodating personality led her to have goods from the marketplace delivered to her cottage so that her presence would not cause discomfort to the vendors or her fellow shoppers.

Which was why, she supposed, she'd become enthralled with Rhys Bloodgood. Not only did he accept her, he seemed to genuinely appreciate her help. As she watched the stern and stoic healer at work in his apothecary, she couldn't help but admire his methodical nature. The wizard adored order and cleanliness. Everything in his apothecary and the attached infirmary had its place. His stringent attention to detail ensured that his patients enjoyed the finest of care in the five kingdoms.

Her respect for his practice was why she'd taken a job working for him at Bloodgood's Apothecary. Once her sister Medea had become queen of Darnuith, they'd sold the fruit farm they'd once managed. Tavyss and Medea had moved in to Maelhaven Palace, as was tradition, and Circe and Isis had moved to a small cottage in Mistcraven, nestled in the Dark Mountains. The apothecary had been a welcome distraction, where her natural inclination for potion making had come in increasingly handy.

It was a safe, prudent, and perfectly acceptable job.

And if her mind sometimes sent her a delicious and perfectly unacceptable fantasy about grabbing her aloof and taciturn boss by the lapels of his laboratory coat and pressing her lips to his, well, there were worse problems to have as a witch.

"Bring me the container marked Mystic Snail Shell,"

he commanded once she'd arrived at his side in his laboratory. The cauldron he hunched over smelled of something sweet and vegetative.

Without hesitation, she jogged into the storage room and searched for what he'd requested. She wasn't exactly sure when she'd become enchanted by Rhys. The waves of his shoulder-length black hair weren't exceptionally silky, and the short beard that muted the hard edge of his jaw looked more rugged than handsome. But she found herself spending more and more time imagining what it would feel like to run a hand down his body, toned from hours of hiking and gathering herbs and roots in the woods. Would Rhys Bloodgood's flesh feel as hard as his personality?

To be sure, the man had done nothing to invite her attentions. He barked orders at her throughout the day. *Sweep the floor. Disinfect the counters. Bring me the forage beetle powder.* There was no softness in his tone or his eyes, and the two of them rarely spoke of personal things. But she sensed that if that icy veneer ever cracked, underneath would be a steaming passion as wild as his waves and as potent as his deep blue stare.

"Circe!"

She rushed back into the lab, carrying the container he'd asked for.

"Place it here," he ordered, pointing to the table beside him. "And be careful to wash your hands. Even a bit of this stuff can befuddle your mind."

Despite knowing she hadn't touched anything but clean, dry glass, Circe left the container beside him and washed her hands in the sink. Still, her mind skipped right over the bossy comment and sent her a lovely vision of sweeping all the herbs and equipment off Rhys's worktable and using its hard surface to crawl on top of him. She'd never had a lover, but she was certain that Rhys would be a thorough and attentive one. If he focused on her with a fraction of the intensity that he gave his work, her blood would positively sing.

A funny swooping feeling happened low in her torso. She shook her head. She was being completely ridiculous.

"What are you working on?" she asked tentatively.

Those piercing blue eyes darted to her, his expression initially annoyed but then morphing into something softer as his gaze swept over her. "Developing an antidote for gila vine poisoning." He gestured toward a potted plant beside the cauldron. "Gila vines are growing out of control along the border of Rogos. Viktor Franwise's sheep keep eating it."

Circe didn't know anything about Rogos, but she remembered Viktor. The elderly man rarely came into the apothecary, preferring to send a falcon to procure Rhys's services. He'd been friendly and kind the last time she'd run into him, though. That was more than she could say about most people here.

Circe sniffed at the gila vine with its variegated, four-pointed leaves and winced. It smelled of anise and something bitter.

Rhys used tongs to drop a few pieces of snail shell into the cauldron. "This ivy is native to the Mystic Wood in Rogos. It's not meant to flourish at higher elevations and hasn't spread into Darnuith in the past. Franwise has been doing his best to keep his sheep away from the stuff. He's moved the herd inland, but the vine is encroaching on his property faster than he can adjust."

"What happens to the sheep when they eat it?"

"The first signs of illness occur about an hour after ingestion. The animals die within twenty-four hours."

"No treatments help?" Circe narrowed her eyes on the vine. "What about inducing vomiting?"

"Doesn't work. Nothing works. Franwise says he's been lucky so far to weed out infected sheep from his herd. Of course, we are both concerned that the poison could make it into the meat supply. No witches or wizards have been harmed by tainted meat thus far, but with the vines coming closer and closer to town, we'd both feel better having a cure on hand."

"Is there no way to contain the vines themselves?"

"Not one with any lasting effectiveness. Rogos is struggling with overgrowth as well this season. I've been working with a scribe there named Daluk on a containment potion, but neither of us has found a permanent solution."

He turned his attention back to his work, and she had to swallow her disappointment. The room seemed to grow colder without the intensity of that gaze on her. Rhys gave his potion three counterclockwise stirs and then nodded as it turned a lighter shade of gray.

"Bring me a narwit," he demanded, without even a glance in her direction.

She retrieved one of the small pink creatures from the cage in the corner. It wiggled its four pink ears at her. With their high metabolism, narwits made the perfect test subjects. Their fast reproduction and short life-span allowed Rhys to collect vast amounts of data quickly. Still, Circe was reluctant to hand the creature over. She did not want to watch it die.

Rhys used the tongs to pluck a leaf from the vine and feed it to the creature, whose tiny nose wrinkled as it chewed. No sooner had the animal swallowed than it fell on its side, its muscles clenching in involuntary spasms.

"Now the antidote." Rhys drew up a dropper of the light-gray elixir and dribbled it into the narwit's mouth. The animal stopped seizing, but its breathing slowed almost to a stop. Rhys put on his work glasses, the ones he'd enchanted to see inside his patients, and examined the creature inside and out. "Fates' fury," he cursed. "It didn't work. It's dying. Heartbeat is barely detectable."

No. Circe couldn't bear to stand by while the creature suffered. She reached out and stroked the leaves of the gila vine, running her fingers along the plant from the base, where the roots disappeared under the soil, over the branches, and along the leaves.

"What are you doing?" Rhys snapped.

She drew her wand and, with a flick of her wrist, sent an analyzing spell over the plant. "This is how I came to understand plants in the Garden of the Hesperides," she said. "Through touch and magical analysis."

Rhys studied her, scowling.

"Of my three sisters, I always had the strongest inclination toward herbs and potions," she explained. "It's inherent in my magic. Transformation is my forte, but in order to transform something, you have to take it apart and put it back together. That's what I'm doing now."

Rhys ran his hands through his hair. "I need that sample, Circe—"

"Oh, I'm not going to take your sample apart. I'm just shining my magic through it to understand it better. For example, the poison does not bleed through the surface of the leaves. One would have to ingest this to be poisoned by it. Touching it is harmless." She glanced at him and smiled.

His brow furrowed. "How do you know that?"

With a swish of her wrist, the light faded. She stowed her wand inside the special pocket built into the sleeve of her tunic. "The same way I know that the reason your potion isn't working is because you need something to warm the blood. You have an analgesic for the pain, an astringent to keep the venom from spreading, and an antidote to neutralize the poison, but this plant kills by dropping its victim's temperature. So, your narwit is suffering from hypothermia while your tonic works to take effect. But the lower temperature has slowed its circulation, making it impossible for its body to make use of the cure."

His mouth worked, but no sound came out.

She left him to rummage in the storeroom. "Aha!" She returned with a jar labeled Pepper of the Valley. Fishing a dark orange pepper from under its lid, she diced it and added it to the brew, stirring the cauldron with six sharp strokes.

Rhys's face was grim, and it occurred to her that it was a good thing she'd moved quickly because if the man hadn't been shocked into inaction, she was sure he'd have kept her from touching his brew. Instantly, the color of the potion changed to a muddy orange and started to bubble. She seized the dropper from Rhys's hand, drew up a dose of the new elixir, and administered it to the narwit.

For a few moments, nothing changed. Rhys's scowl grew darker.

The narwit rocked, then scrambled to its feet, blinking and wiggling its nose. Circe grinned.

Rhys's eyebrows climbed in increments to his hairline. He donned his enchanted glasses again and examined the narwit's internal happenings. "Remarkable. Circe, you've done it!"

Circe flourished her hand and took a bow. "Glad I could help."

He removed his glasses and locked eyes with her. Again, the intensity of his stare made her knees wobble, but this time she saw more in his expression. The corner of his mouth turned up in a hint of a smile that made his eyes crinkle at the corners. Rhys never smiled. That twist of lip made her feel important. Vital. Like her heart had never beat before he'd gazed in her direction. She had to remember to breathe.

"You truly are a brilliant and gifted witch, Circe."

"Th-thank you," she stammered.

He stepped closer to her, until mere inches remained between them, and the slightly herbal scent of his skin filled her nose. She doubted he was the type to wear cologne and thought it must be his soap or the remnants of the herbs he gathered every morning. *Ugh*, he was so handsome. That curl that persistently teased his forehead no matter how many times he tucked the rest of his hair behind his ears drove her mad, and the deep blue of his eyes was worthy of drowning in.

"I'm very lucky to have you here," he said softly, his attention drifting to her lips. "I meant what I said before about wanting you to stay. I need you here, no matter how many windows those bastards break."

She allowed the intense connection between them to draw her forward another fraction of an inch. His lips were full, and he looked at her from under impossibly long lashes. He leaned forward. Circe's heart thudded in her chest. Was he going to kiss her?

The front door chimed, and Rhys started as if waking from a dream. He blinked rapidly. "You should get that."

"Oh, uh, of course." She slid past him and hurried to the front desk, where she was surprised to find a man in a royal tunic. It was not unheard of for Darnuith's soldiers to seek treatment there, but this man did not appear ill.

"Circe Tanglewood?" he asked her.

"Yes?"

He held out an ornate purple envelope with a red wax seal pressed with an insignia in the shape of the Tanglewood tree—her sister's seal. She accepted the envelope from the soldier.

"What is this?" she asked.

"An invitation to a royal banquet. The queen sends her love." He bowed and headed for the door.

"Wait!" Circe raised a hand and smiled when the soldier looked her way. "Please tell Medea I love her too, and I wouldn't miss it."

He'd almost kissed her. Rhys tipped his head back and groaned toward the ceiling of his laboratory. Of all the stupid things he could have done! Thank the Fates the door had chimed when it had, or he might be in a terrible mess. A kiss would have been a disaster.

He swept the narwit off the table and returned it to its cage, where it squeaked and ran in circles. Circe was the queen's sister and a gifted employee. So talented that one day he might even make her his apprentice. He'd be a fool to enter into a romantic relationship with her. One false move and he could lose the best thing to happen to his apothecary in years, or worse, should his actions displease the queen, he could lose his head. And that didn't even begin to encompass the blowback he'd get from the residents of Mistcraven for dating one of the three sisters. He'd already been pulled aside by more than one well-meaning friend to warn him about hiring her. Anything more and he'd never hear the end of it.

No, the last thing he should be doing was kissing Circe.

He straightened his lab coat and composed himself before striding to the front of his apothecary to see who'd come in. A man in a royal uniform was halfway out the door. "What was that all about?"

Circe stood at the counter holding a purple envelope with the royal seal. She frowned at the card within. "An invitation from my sister," she said absently. "She's throwing a royal dinner party."

"A royal banquet?" He raised an eyebrow. "Seems like a joyous occasion. Why are you looking at it like you want to set it on fire?"

She smiled at him. That smile held the sun. For a moment, his brain blanked trying to process the beauty of it. Then he swallowed hard and busied himself straightening a box of healing crystals.

"It requires that I bring a guest." A gusty sigh left her lungs. "I don't want to turn Medea down. She's been so lonely since she became queen. But I'm not sure I can do this."

"Are you suggesting that the queen will not allow her own sister to attend her dinner party without a date?" Rhys tried to make light of the situation. Surely it wasn't as dire as Circe made it sound.

Circe chewed her lip before speaking. "Medea spends too much time locked up in that palace. To elevate her boredom, she's become enchanted with party games, especially Royal Cross. She thinks it's delightful to play teams, which requires an even number of guests. She's gone so far as to mention it in the invitation. If I don't bring a guest, it will throw off the players. Even if I sat the game out, it would leave a spot open on the board."

As much as he'd love to tell her she was wrong and her participation didn't matter, Rhys was familiar with Royal Cross; he used to excel at the game as a child. It was played on a field divided into four quadrants by crossed lines of stones. Each quadrant was divided into six sectors. Each sector contained an object that could only be manipulated by magic. The object of the game was to move all the objects out of your quadrant into your opponent's quadrant. Each team got one turn to analyze and move their object while also spelling it to make it harder for the opposing team to move back. Each item had its own hidden properties at the start of the game which made it more challenging to manipulate. It took logic, strategy, and power to win. Circe hadn't misinterpreted the invitation.

"Why does this upset you? For a woman like you, I'm sure finding a guest shouldn't be too difficult." Rhys couldn't help but scowl as he said it. Circe was a beautiful woman. He'd noticed many men watching her with hungry eyes when they'd journeyed into town for healing visits. Not only was she beautiful enough to put the grandest mountain views of Darnuith to shame, the power to be gained by a relationship with the queen's sister would appeal to many of his sex.

Many of the *wrong* type of men, he supposed. *Fates' fury.* He made an effort to keep his expression impassive. As much as it would be mischief to pursue Circe, he did not like to think about her attending a banquet with another man, especially with one who entertained dark motives.

"You're wrong about it not being difficult," she said sadly. "You saw what happened this morning. Half of Darnuith hates us. They've never accepted my sister as the true queen. I can't even invite a girlfriend because I have none other than Isis, and she's invited as well. No one speaks to me except for a curt hello or goodbye. The few men I've met who initially seem interested are often intimidated by me."

He hated how dejected she looked. Were those tears in her eyes? He didn't think he could stand to see her cry. The thought awakened a deep protective instinct in him he hadn't felt in a very long time.

"That can't be true," he assured her, although the thought of her wanting for male attention made him oddly joyful inside. "There must be someone you could ask."

"Rhys?"

"Yes?" His brows climbed. Was she thinking about asking him? Folly.

She sighed and spread her arms wide. "In your professional opinion, is there something wrong with me? Something offensive that causes the people here to push me away?"

"No!" he said a little too forcefully, but he just couldn't leave her believing that. "If people here seem reluctant to trust you, it's only because outsiders are rare in Darnuith and it is unheard of for a witch from another land to become queen. It's unsettling to the older families who came to expect the Fates to do the same thing they'd always done. Give it time. People will open their hearts and minds." It wasn't a lie. He'd heard scattered whisperings of how pleased people were with Medea's rule. The hatred Circe had witnessed wasn't universal, as much as it'd seemed so.

She took a step toward him. "Really? You're not just saying that?"

The corner of his mouth twitched of its own accord despite his brain screaming that he should under no circumstances be wooing Circe with kind words. "I wouldn't say it if it weren't true. I hate liars."

Her hand came to rest on top of his, and she squeezed his fingers. The tension he'd felt during the almost kiss in the laboratory seized him again, and his brain flashed a delicious vision of lifting her onto the counter, shoving up her dress, and spreading her thighs. He turned away from her to hide the lust that must be evident in his eyes.

"If you'll excuse me..." He moved for the storage room, putting precious space between them. A woman had no business being so enchanting. Every time he looked at her, he lost his damned mind.

"Rhys?"

He ignored her and started moving jars around like he was truly busy, when the apothecary was as tidy as it had ever been.

She came up behind him, her presence like a live flame in the small room. Her spirit could not be ignored. He cleared his throat and met her gaze.

"Would *you* go with me?"

He stopped. He could feel a scowl pass through his

expression, and a sharp pain flared across Circe's features in response. She looked as if he'd struck her, and he hadn't said a word.

"Forget I asked," she added quickly, her voice soft and thready. "I... I don't know what I was thinking—"

"I'll go with you," he blurted. The words were out of his mouth before he could think it through. Anything to make her smile again.

Her face brightened, sending warmth through him. "Thank you. Oh, Rhys, thank you." She backed toward the front of the store again, and he took a deep breath of fresh air.

"As your friend, of course," he added toward her back. "Anything else would be inappropriate, considering we work together."

At first, she looked shocked. Then her eyes narrowed and her smile faded. She nodded in agreement. "O-of course," she sputtered. "As a favor to me. I'll owe you one."

Rhys grabbed a few empty jars and shoved them into the bag he used to collect specimens. With a few terse words that served as a goodbye, he escaped out the door. He'd made a date with Circe. As friends. He rolled his eyes toward the heavens as he mounted his broom. An evening with her would either be a whiff of heaven or a stroll through hell. He wasn't sure he was ready for either.

THREE

Circe fastened the waist of her gown and wondered if it was too much. Rhys had made it clear that tonight they were attending her sister's banquet as friends, a confusing notion considering she was sure he'd been close to kissing her. She'd wanted him to kiss her. She'd been drawn to him from the first time she'd walked into Bloodgood's Apothecary.

The dress she was wearing could never be described as friendly. If the energy of a deep kiss was turned into fabric and wrapped around her, it would look like this dress. She'd found it in the window of a clothier in Mistcraven. The witch who ran the shop made alterations to accommodate Circe's above-average height and willowy stature. The deep rose-colored fabric skimmed her torso before flaring out in featherlight layers from her hips. For some reason, the color made her eyes turn a deeper blue. Not as dark as Isis's, whose irises could appear black under certain light, but a richer shade like the inside of a sapphire.

What would Rhys say? Would he take one look at her and know she'd lied about only wanting his friendship? Would he be reluctant to go with her once he saw her?

She shook her head. She was being ridiculous. The gown was perfectly appropriate for a royal banquet, and despite what she might think when she looked at him, he couldn't see inside her soul or read her mind, not even with his enchanted glasses.

A knock came on her bedroom door, and she opened it to find her sister Isis, resplendent in a royal-blue sheath dress. "The carriage is here. The driver picked up the men first. How much do you want to bet that Brody has blood somewhere on his person?"

Circe smiled. Isis had fallen in with a group of hunters early on and, despite being the only female among their ranks, was the most prolific with a bow and arrow. Her date for this event was a wizard and fellow hunter named Brody who'd been trying to woo her for months.

"I thought you mentioned you weren't interested in Brody?"

"I'm not. He was the only one I could find on short notice. And what about Rhys? Does he know you want to wed him and have his babies?" Isis's eyes twinkled with laughter.

"Bite your tongue. He made it clear today he only cares to be friends."

Isis pressed a finger into the crook of her chin. "Has he seen you in that dress?"

Circe shook her head.

Isis's eyes darkened to midnight blue. "I predict he

might change his mind by the end of the night. You'll gorgonize him with a single wink."

Cheeks hot, Circe grabbed her bag and pushed through the door. "Don't be obtuse. I'm perfectly common."

"If you say so."

She and Isis made their way out to the carriage, where a royal escort waited to help them inside. Unlike the carriages she'd read about in books that were built atop wheels, this one, like all carriages in Darnuith, was built atop sled skis. Most of Darnuith's roads were permanently frozen, and the skis were enchanted to slide over all manner of ground, even rough or rocky terrain. Pulled by a team of tall, shaggy dogs with red eyes called vultar hounds, the carriage was a more comfortable way to travel than by broom when an event required formal dress.

As she stepped up into the carriage, the hounds panted at her from their harnesses, buzzing with an overflowing energy and the inborn desire to pull. She slid into the seat next to Isis with her back facing the driver and greeted Rhys and Brody.

"Fates alive, you two are stunning," Brody said, his eyes darting between them. "Are you sure it's safe to outshine the queen?"

Circe laughed. "If you think anything about us outshines our sister, you haven't met Medea."

Rhys's eyes flicked over her. He frowned as if her appearance displeased him. Grumpily, he turned his face toward the window. Circe's heart crushed itself into a tight little ball at the snub.

"You have blood on your sock," Isis said, pointing to the edge of Brody's shoe, which did indeed sport a dark splotch.

He shrugged. "Elderbeast." Unceremoniously, he blotted it with his handkerchief, then returned the bloody square of fabric to his pocket. Isis glanced at Circe and chuckled.

The rest of the ride was ominously quiet. Tension bled off Rhys and seemed to put all four of them in a foul mood. It was hard to be jovial with a dark cloud looming nearby. Whatever offense she'd committed, no matter how unintentional, must have been heinous in his eyes.

She decided to confront him about it once they were alone.

The carriage came to a stop before the golden doors of Maelhaven Palace. The driver opened the carriage and escorted them inside.

"Finally!" Medea rushed Circe in a way that was all about familial bonds and probably completely inappropriate for a royal. She embraced her and then Isis. Behind her, Tavyss, Medea's husband and mate, smiled. The dragon's gold eyes shone bright as he watched her sister. Tavyss was happy when Medea was happy, and the three sisters were happiest with their arms wrapped around one another.

"My queen, the Royal Cross board is ready for you in the ballroom," Zelaria announced. The adviser to the queen wore a roomy deep-purple dress with a feathery shawl that was as wispy as her wild gray hair. When the Fates had chosen Medea, Circe feared Zelaria would be bitter or would abscond herself of her role. But Medea claimed she'd been a remarkable help in establishing her rule.

"Don't you mean ready for us?" Medea asked. "You and Tamsin still plan to play the fourth quadrant, I hope."

Zelaria leaned on her staff. "We wouldn't miss it."

"Good," Tavyss said. "Because Medea requires Cook to wait until the game is played before serving the food, and I'm hungry. At least I know with this talented lot, it will be a short game."

Circe fell behind and sidled up to Rhys as the others filtered into the ballroom. "Is it just me, or do you have the feeling we're going to lose this game abysmally? I've never even played."

He lowered his voice. "We won't lose. I'll show you what to do." His eyes darted over her again, and the scowl from the carriage snapped back into place.

"Have I done something wrong? Is my dress offensive to you? I've only lived in Darnuith a year. I'm not familiar with all of your customs, but the woman in the shop said this would be appropriate."

"There's nothing wrong with you or your dress, Circe," he said through a grimace.

"Then why are you scowling at me?"

"Come on, you two!" Medea called. "The game awaits."

Rhys avoided her question and gestured toward the ballroom. He did not escort her as they made their way inside, even though it was customary for partners to enter arm in arm. Based on the gruff energy coming off the man, she'd definitely read him wrong days ago when she'd thought he might kiss her. Clearly, he was not interested. He looked as if he didn't even want to be there.

She followed him to the third quadrant and stood inside her ring. In front of her, there was a feather, a stone, a large crystal, a potted sapling, a silver chalice filled with water, and a red wax candle that flickered at her from its sector. She studied the objects, trying to come up with a strategy. As painful as it was, she had no choice but to engage with Rhys again. He was the one who understood how to play.

"Shouldn't the feather be the easiest to move?" Circe asked him. "I can simply levitate it over the line into Isis and Brody's quadrant."

Rhys scoffed. "It is, but it is also the easiest for them to move back, as well as the other item whose sector you put it in. Also, feathers are extremely hard to layer with enchantment. Their nature is to remain pure."

"What do you recommend?"

He raised an eyebrow at her. "The tree, of course. Green magic has always been my strength."

Of course. He owned an apothecary, for Fates' sake. She lowered her voice. "The tree it is. We'll go with your strengths first. As for me, I'm fairly good with water and earth elements, but transformation is my specialty."

"So I've witnessed."

From across the field, Medea whistled to get their attention. "We draw to see who goes first." A servant entered the room carrying an ornate gold box. "The coins are numbered. Number one makes the first move."

The servant approached Circe, and she drew a coin. "Two," she announced.

"That's a good position," Rhys said. "It allows us to react to the first couple's strategy."

"One," Zelaria said. Her partner, Tamsin, was already studying the board, his knuckle pressed to his chin.

"Very well," Medea said. "You go first. House rules are that you get one move to layer as many spells as you can execute at one time. The only requirement is that you must restore the nature of your object to its original state and move it at least one square before you add any other elements to the mix."

"What does that mean?" Circe asked Rhys. "Restore the nature of your object?"

He laughed. "It means if a competitor freezes the water in the chalice, we have to melt it back into water before we can move it or enchant it ourselves. It sounds simple enough, but remember, we must do it in one layered spell. Any more than four layers and things become... unpredictable."

No kidding. Circe wasn't sure she'd ever done a spell like that in her life.

Medea dropped a red silk ribbon on the floor to signal the start of the game, and Zelaria floated her feather over Medea's candle. It burst into flames and rained ash into the sector. Circe grimaced, finally understanding the game. Now Medea would have to restore the feather before moving both feather and candle.

"Our turn," Rhys said. "I'm second-guessing our plan. Do you trust me to make the first move?" Their eyes met, and she was back in his laboratory, his lips so close to her own.

She couldn't help gazing at his mouth as she answered. "Yes, please."

Rhys drew his wand and floated the heavy stone over Isis's sapling, raising it high into the air before allowing it to drop on the plant. Its branches flattened to the floor.

"That's it, Bloodgood. The gloves are coming off!" After an exchange of whispers with Isis, Brody moved their chalice into Circe's candle sector, and the water sloshed over the rim, dousing the flame.

"Easy enough to fix," Rhys whispered.

The game continued, and soon it was clear that each team had their strengths and weaknesses. Medea was a master spellcaster, able to consistently layer five spells at once, but as a dragon, her partner Tavyss could contribute only fire and a very simple protective ward. Isis and Brody were particularly good with setting traps, for example, enchanting the crystal to shatter after the next move, but they were terrible at green magic and lost a turn trying to heal the sapling Rhys had destroyed. Zelaria and Tamsin managed some truly creative fire and water spells, at one point tunneling the water into the stone, which proved a puzzle that thwarted Medea for three moves, but they struggled with defensive magic.

Unsurprisingly, Circe and Rhys excelled with plants and water as well as strategy, but they often fell for Isis's traps. After dozens of moves, however, it was clear that Zelaria and Tamsin were in the lead with only the rock and crystal left in the same sector of their quadrant. Rhys and Circe were in second place, with three objects in two sectors, the sapling in one and the crystal and the feather in another. It was their turn.

"I have an idea," Circe whispered. "But I'm not sure if it's against the rules." She cupped her hand and whispered it into Rhys's ear.

"Brilliant," he said. "Do it."

She raised her wand and, with an intricate pattern of interlocking swirls, transformed the sapling into a rock badger. The creature walked into the neighboring sector, shoved the crystal and feather into its marsupial pouch, and then bound into Zelaria's quadrant where it curled up and fell asleep.

Medea beamed at her. "You've done it! Your quadrant is empty. You've won the game."

But Zelaria shook her head. "Foul play! The rules clearly state that competitors can enchant the objects in one sector only."

Circe laughed. "I did. My transfiguration was of the sapling, layered with a mind-control spell to suggest to the rock badger what I wanted it to do. Once it left my sector, it was on its own."

"I believe there is no rule against it," Medea said. "I declare Circe and Rhys my winners!"

FOUR

Rhys was disappointed when Zelaria and Tamsin turned their backs and marched away from the board without even offering them congratulations. Poor sports. It was a solid game and all in good fun. But then, Zelaria looked like she hadn't smiled in years, and her partner was equally melancholy.

In an effort to lighten the mood, he shook hands with the queen, Tavyss, Isis, and Brody and complimented each of them thoroughly. "Brilliantly played!"

Only after the group started for the dining room did he face Circe. He should compliment her play as well, but Fates, he could hardly look at her in that dress. Her beauty threatened to burn him. He'd respected her from the day she'd started working for him. It was clear from the beginning she had a strong work ethic and was honorable and trustworthy. Now that she'd shown him she was also a talented witch, he desired her more than ever—and that was before she'd gone and put on a dress that skimmed every curve and put her breasts on display.

A woman had no business being that lovely, intelligent, and talented. He thought his heart might leap through his chest and ask her to dance.

But it was a terrible idea to pursue Circe. Most of Darnuith was circumspect when it came to Medea's reign. He heard the whispers. The Fates may have selected her as queen, but the people hadn't welcomed her with open arms. All three sisters were still considered outsiders.

And while his fellow witches and wizards might forgive him for giving her a job, he understood it would be an uphill battle if he courted her. His apothecary counted on the trust and loyalty of Mistcraven's witches and wizards.

Not that anyone else's opinion would stop him if there weren't more to the equation. He'd take the risk if there wasn't the chance that Queen Medea would find him lacking. Plus, everyone would be watching—or trying to anyway. Disappoint Circe, and things could get awful for him. He hated politics, but it was an unquestionable truth. The scrutiny that would come with a relationship with Circe was not something he wanted to sign up for.

Oh, who was he kidding? None of that would be enough to keep him from her if he weren't a damned coward. It was reliving the past he feared most. He pushed that bit down deep. He couldn't face it. Not now.

"We should join the others in the dining room," she said. He'd been so lost in thought that he hadn't even noticed the room had cleared out and they were now alone. She gave him a sidelong look, her fingers tangled in front of her hips. "Rhys... is everything okay?"

He'd been a complete asshole to her this entire night. If nothing else, he had to set things straight. "Circe... I should have told you before, your dress is lovely. Please don't take my foul mood personally. It has more to do with me than with you."

He gave her a curt nod, then turned on his heel and headed for the dining room.

"Oh no, you don't," Circe blurted. She caught up to him and turned him by the elbow. "What does that even mean? Three days ago, I thought we... shared a moment, and then you made it clear you only wanted a friendship. Fine, but then you see me and treat me like you either hate me or are offended by me. Aside from the game, which you did seem to enjoy, I thought you were counting down the seconds in your head of how long you had to spend with me. Please explain how this is all about you and not me? Because where I'm standing, it feels personal."

He took a deep breath and blew it out, the tension in his face and shoulders going with it. Everything about her drew him in. The soft blush of her cheeks, the intense blue of her eyes, the way she held her spine straight and her chin up. She was no wilting flower. His behavior may have confused her, even hurt her, but she knew her worth and wanted answers.

He licked his lips and planned to say something vague like wanting to keep a professional distance or it not being the right time, but somehow, the only thing that came out was the one thing he hadn't wanted to share, almost as if her presence was a talisman designed to elicit the truth.

"I was married once," he said, his throat thick with bygone memories. "When I look at you, it reminds me of what it was to feel something. And I just can't risk that again."

This time when he strode away, she let him go.

WHY HAD HE MENTIONED JUNE? Rhys pushed his food around his plate with his fork, regretting the sudden onslaught of honesty. It made no sense. He hadn't wanted to think about it. Hades, it was ancient history. Now there was no taking it back.

Beside him, Circe was carrying on a conversation with her sisters as if the revelation hadn't fazed her one bit. He listened in, hoping none of her words were about her moody and temperamental boss.

"How long can you put it off?" Circe asked the queen.

Medea squeezed Tavyss's hand. "As long as I have to. I'm the queen."

"Put what off?" Rhys mumbled.

"Eleanor and Brynhoff of Paragon have sent multiple invitations to the palace. They want to meet the new witch queen of Darnuith. But if they agree to a meeting, it's going to cause complications," Circe said.

"No one outside Darnuith knows Medea's mate is a dragon," Zelaria said, a note of gossip in her voice. "Or that he is the eldest brother of the king and queen of Paragon."

The clank of Rhys's fork hitting his plate seemed to echo in the room. "Sorry," he mumbled, regripping the utensil. He'd known Tavyss was a dragon but wasn't aware of his royal ties to Paragon. If he was the eldest heir, the Paragonian throne was rightfully his. What were he and Medea even doing here?

"There's no reason for us to go," Tavyss said to Circe over his wine. "We don't owe Paragon anything."

Zelaria waved a finger in his direction. "How can you suggest such a thing? A queen must have a relationship with neighboring territories. We have trade routes to consider. Access to the Sanguine River. Paragonian imports. If you refuse Eleanor's royal invitation again, it will strain diplomatic relations to the breaking point. The damage might already be done, frankly. Paragon will assume you are planning war."

Medea frowned. "I'll send an envoy. We'll simply explain that domestic concerns in Darnuith are my top priority at the moment. Tavyss's identity will remain confidential. I will stay here."

"If you cared at all about Paragon, you would find a way to go," Zelaria said.

Rhys cleared his throat. "I have to agree with Zelaria on this one," he said softly. "Several plants and herbs we use for healing only grow in the volcanic soil of Paragon. Many lives are saved every year through their application. Our access to them has always depended on a civil relationship at the border."

The enormity of what he'd learned tonight about Tavyss continued to fester at the back of Rhys's mind. Did Circe even understand the tightrope her sister was walking? As the eldest brother to Eleanor and Brynhoff, Tavyss's role as Medea's consort would be considered suspicious. All the rumors about the invalidity of the Sacred Lots, that the three sisters had somehow used magic to change the outcome, would explode once Tavyss's identity was widely known. His presence would definitely cause friction with the other kingdoms, especially if there was any fear that he'd exercise his right to the Paragonian throne.

No amount of avoidance would keep this secret forever. How many others in Darnuith already knew the truth? If Zelaria knew, likely a few. The woman had never been skilled at keeping a secret. Surely any fears could be assuaged with diplomacy. Couldn't Medea see that avoidance and secrecy were making things worse?

Circe glanced between her sisters and then focused on Tavyss. "What if Tavyss stayed here? Medea, you and Zelaria could go, or take one of us."

Medea didn't meet her sister's eyes but instead stared down at her hands.

"It's more complicated than you're making it out to be," Tavyss said. "There are things you don't know, reasons why it might not be safe for Medea to travel now. Things only the Fates can control."

"What sorts of things?" Isis asked, her dark eyes narrowing on her sister. Rhys got the distinct impression that the witch had made a deal with the darkness at some point in her life. Night seemed to leach from her skin.

Rhys glanced back at Medea and Tavyss, who were staring at each other as if they didn't quite know if they should answer. Medea's mouth twitched into a smile, but Tavyss gave a sharp shake of his head. What secrets were they keeping?

Finally, they seemed to come to some agreement. Medea gestured to a servant, and the man poured a bubbly drink into each of their glasses. Rhys sniffed it. Thornberry wine. Very rare. What was this all about?

Medea stood and raised her glass. "What I'm about to tell you now is strictly confidential," she said. "It's very early, and we had not intended to share the news so soon."

Everyone silenced. The entire room seemed to be holding its collective breath.

"Tavyss and I are going to have a baby."

Beside him, Zelaria gasped.

"Congratulations!" Circe stood to reach across the table and tap her glass to Medea's and then Tavyss's. Her action led everyone else to do the same, including Rhys, although inside, his shoulders tensed and he ground his teeth. Not everyone would be happy about this revelation. Things would undoubtedly get more difficult for Circe and her sisters once news of the pregnancy got out.

Zelaria raised her glass. "To Medea and Tavyss and the future of the kingdom of Darnuith."

Everyone drank.

Rhys lowered his glass, distracted by the queen. She was trembling, one hand rising to her throat.

"What's happening?" Tavyss reached for her.

Medea collapsed into his arms, twitching violently.

"Medea!" Circe knocked over her chair getting around the table to her sister. "I need to examine her."

Tavyss lowered her to the floor. Circe drew her wand but didn't need to use it. An acrid scent met her nose when she leaned over Medea. She brought her face close to Medea's mouth, then straightened and sniffed her glass. She knew that scent. Fates' fury! "Anise and something bitter... Rhys, it's gila vine! She's been poisoned!"

Zelaria's eyes widened. "Impossible!"

"We have to get her to my apothecary," Rhys yelled. "Bring the carriage!"

"What can you do? There's no antidote," Zelaria said, sounding distraught.

Circe cursed. How could the damned witch be so heartless? That wasn't what Tavyss needed to hear right now.

"There is a cure," Rhys said. "But we must act fast."

Tavyss swept Medea into his arms, and they raced for

the carriage. Circe, Rhys, and Isis squeezed in, but there wasn't room for Zelaria, Brody, and Tamsin, who gracefully stayed behind. The driver whipped the hounds into a frenzy, and Circe clung to the edge of her seat to keep from flying into Rhys at every turn. It didn't seem fast enough. Her stomach clenched with every twitch and shiver that racked Medea's body.

No sooner had the carriage come to a halt than Rhys took command. He ordered Tavyss to bring Medea to the infirmary while he raced to the storage room for the elixir they'd developed.

"Hold her!"

Circe did as he commanded, tipping her sister's head back so that her mouth popped open. Rhys dribbled the orange sludge into her mouth, then dropped the empty vial on the counter. Medea's mouth started to foam, and her eyes rolled back in her head.

"What's happening?" Tavyss demanded.

Rhys backed away from the dragon whose voice had lowered to an animal growl. "It's normal. The antidote has to neutralize the poison. It's going to look scary for a moment, but it will work."

Circe hoped he was right. They'd never tested the antidote on a human. She refused to think of the many things that could go wrong. This was Medea's only hope.

As Medea's body went rigid, Circe met Isis's dark gaze. Shadows reached from the corners of the room toward her. Isis didn't have to say a word for Circe to know exactly what she was thinking. If anything happened to Medea or the baby, the two of them would hunt down whoever did this and kill them. No one hurt their sister. No one.

Tenderly, Tavyss stroked the hair back from Medea's face and pressed his lips to her temple. "Fight, my love. You can do this."

Gradually, Medea's mouth stopped foaming and her muscles relaxed.

Rhys cleaned her face with a wet towel and pressed his fingers to the side of her neck. "Her pulse is strong. I think we're beyond the worst of it."

Relief flooded Circe. He'd done it. They'd done it. The admiration she felt for Rhys made her want to pull him into her arms.

Medea squeezed her hand. Circe tore her gaze away from Rhys and settled it on Medea. The queen's eyes blinked open. "What happened?"

"You were poisoned!" Circe cried. "Thank the Fates Rhys had a cure."

She made room for Tavyss to pull Medea into his arms. He wrapped his wings around her. Scales broke out along his arms, and his eyes glowed with yellow fire. A growl rattled in his throat. At times like these, it was impossible to forget that Tavyss was a dragon and Medea was his greatest treasure.

"Tavyss? Tavyss, I'm fine." Medea pressed a hand against his heart.

Wanting to give them privacy, Circe turned away. Rhys was standing outside the door, shoulders sagging. He looked exhausted but also...relieved. Both of them knew the entire situation could have gone another way.

She joined him outside the infirmary and whispered, "You did it. It worked. It's okay."

"Thanks to you." His gaze bore into hers. "If it wasn't for your magic and your brilliant mind, she'd be dead. People here, they don't realize what they have in you."

The intensity of being the sole object of Rhys's attention was almost too much. She resisted the urge to look away. Was he talking about the people of Darnuith or someone far closer to home? A ghost of a smile raised her cheeks. "Thank you. I'm just happy that it worked."

He nodded. "There's one more patient we need to check."

Circe froze. "The baby!"

From the laboratory, Rhys retrieved his enchanted glasses and stepped back into the room. With some prodding and explanation, Circe was able to convince Tavyss to let Rhys examine Medea once more. He stared at her abdomen while Circe held her breath.

"He's fine," Rhys blurted, his gaze finding hers and a rare smile dancing fleetingly across his face. Circe watched the tension ease from his body, and her heart thumped with joy. For a moment, it was as if they were the only two people in the room, bathing in the realization that something they'd created together had saved her sister's life, her baby's life.

"He?" Medea asked, breaking the intense connection.

"He," Rhys confirmed, turning his smile on the queen.

Circe grinned at her sister. Isis wrapped her arms around Medea and Tavyss, pressing her forehead to the side of Medea's head.

"You should stay here tonight," Rhys said to Medea and Tavyss. "Just for the night. In case there are any side effects."

Circe nodded her agreement. She had another reason for wanting Medea to stay in the infirmary tonight. They still didn't know who in the palace had poisoned her.

Seeming to read her thoughts, Isis came closer, her eyes shadowed with dark thoughts. "We will find who did this, sister," she said softly, just to her.

Circe nodded. "Yes, we will."

LATER THAT EVENING, Circe struggled to find a reason not to go home. Medea and Tavyss were sleeping peacefully in the infirmary. Isis had left hours ago. But something kept her there, waiting in the front room of the apothecary, in a chair reserved for family members. Part of it was wanting to keep her sister safe. But there was something else, too. Something she couldn't quite put her finger on.

"I thought you'd gone home." Rhys stood in the doorway to his laboratory, eyes puffy with fatigue.

"I couldn't bring myself to go. I just want to know that she's okay."

He rubbed his eyes with his thumb and forefinger. "She's going to be fine. And I just finished brewing another batch of antidote in case anyone else in the palace is poisoned."

Circe frowned. "It was meant for her. All of us drank

the wine, and she was the only one who suffered ill effects. Someone on the inside wants her dead.”

“I think so too, but you can never be too careful. Tavyss told me he ordered Zelaria to interrogate every person who touched Medea’s glass. Every member of the Royal Guard is searching the grounds for clues in case someone snuck in from the outside.”

Who would do such a thing to her sister? Circe was too tired to even think about it.

“Why didn’t you tell me before about your wife?” she asked. That was it. The other reason she’d stayed. It nagged at her like a persistent itch, and only now, with him here in front of her, did she realize how much it bothered her.

She hadn’t planned to bring it up, but Fates, she had to know. What had happened to her? It must have ended badly.

“It’s not something I like to talk about.” He glanced out the window toward the stars, bright in the night sky.

“Where is she now? Is it someone I know? Someone from Mistcraven?”

He blinked rapidly at her. “The Glade Cemetery,” he said softly. “I am widowed, ten years now.”

Her mouth dropped open. She hadn’t expected that. He was so young. “I’m sorry.”

He shrugged and tilted his head as if to acknowledge she couldn’t have known. “June was the reason I started Bloodgood’s. She died from a rare fever the old healer, Merriweather, couldn’t cure. Merriweather used magic more than medicine, and after I buried her, I made it my mission to understand how the gifts of the Fates, herbs and roots, could augment spells and enchantments in the healing process. If June were dying today, I'd be able to save her."

"Oh, Rhys." She placed a hand on her chest. "Was that why you were upset today? Did you feel like you were betraying your wife's memory by attending the game with me?"

He jerked, shaking his head. "No. I came to terms with her death years ago, Circe."

"Then what was it? When I climbed into that carriage, you looked at me like I was covered in vilt dung. I know you said we can only be friends, but friends don't treat friends that way. Even Brody paid me a compliment."

He scoffed. "But that's the problem." He strode closer to her and held out his hand. She placed her fingers into his. With a tug, he pulled her onto her feet so that she stood only inches from him. "I don't think I can be your friend."

She gasped.

He pressed a finger over her lips.

"When I saw you today in this dress..." His gaze raked over her as if he could see down to her bones, all her inner workings, even without his enchanted glasses. "Every part of me wanted you, Circe. For the first time since my wife's death, I wanted someone to be mine in every way. I want your mind, your body, your soul." His voice turned gritty and sent a shiver along her skin. He stepped in a little closer and took a lock of her dark hair between his fingers, stroking it near her shoulder. "I shouldn't be telling you this. I think the exhaustion is working as a truth serum. I can't seem to keep it to myself anymore. I feel something for you that I haven't felt in a long time, and it scares me. It scares me to death."

Circe's heart swelled at the admission. He was a widower, still scarred by his wife's death. "It's okay. I understand. I'd never rush you. We don't have to—"

He pulled her against him, one arm banding her waist like a vise. "I wanted to kiss you that day in the laboratory. I did. But a kiss is a magical thing, Circe. It's a doorway, and once you pass through it, you've always been kissed and you've always done the kissing, and nothing is sadder than a kiss that was but can never be again. Don't you know that in this dress, you are like a walking kiss? You are bright and hot and begging to be tasted, and here you are in my arms like a dream."

"If it is a dream, you should lower your voice so that we don't wake up." Her fingers tangled in his hair. "Kisses are magic, but not such a rare kind to never be had again. So, kiss me, Rhys. Kiss me, and then kiss me again. I won't go up in smoke."

He shook his head. "But nothing lasts forever. I, of all people, know that and know the pain of an unexpected ending."

"But do you know the pain of unrequited love? A broken egg will never be a chick. If a kiss is a door, then only by having it can you see what's on the other side. Nothing lasts forever. You said it yourself. I'll take every door that's offered. I wouldn't want to miss a chance."

She rose up onto her toes, brought her lips close to his. At his advantaged height, he'd have to bend his neck a little more for their lips to meet. She waited, feeling his hesitancy in the stiff posture of his back. His navy eyes glinted in the moonlight, wild as if he were warring with himself.

All the tension bled from him on a sigh. "Forgive me."

"There's nothing to forgive."

His mouth pressed against hers then, lips gentle and warm, the edge of his beard soft against her chin. She'd never been kissed before. Not like this, anyway. She tipped her head and gave herself over to it. His tongue dipped between her lips, stroked along her tongue. She could feel that kiss all the way to her toes, but especially in the tips of her breasts and deep within her core.

She wrapped her arms around his neck and pressed herself against him. She wanted him. Wanted more.

But he gently pushed her away, his breath coming in trembling pants.

"What's wrong?" she asked.

"Absolutely nothing," he said. "There's so much right about that kiss I'm surprised we haven't both gone up in flames."

She laughed. Her cheeks and ears grew hot.

"We're both tired," he said around a smile. "There will be other days, other kisses, other nights."

She nodded. "Yes."

"Then let's leave the door open for now and savor the view."

She took a step back, her fingers trailing from his. "I like that idea."

"I should escort you home. You don't have your broom. You'll have to walk."

She bit her lip and shook her head. "My cottage is close. I need some cool night air anyway."

He winked. "Tomorrow, Circe."

"Tomorrow."

She slipped out the door into the night.

SIX

"Where is my queen? I have news."

Rhys stared across the counter at Zelaria. He'd always thought the witch reminded him of a dead tree come to life. She wasn't old by any means. Under fifty, he estimated. But her skin was sallow and weathered, and her hair fell in frizzy coils to her shoulders.

Years ago, he'd thought she could have been beautiful. Could have been. But any beauty the Fates had given her was wasted on her. She rarely smiled, and when she did, as she was doing now, there was no warmth to it.

"She's in the infirmary. Tavyss is in there with her. I'll show you back." He started in Medea's direction, but Zelaria held up a hand. "No need."

She strode past him, her staff tapping the floor between every step. Power radiated off that staff. Unquestionable power. And just like with her smile, Rhys thought there was no warmth in her magic, no heart. Maybe that was why the Fates had not chosen her to be queen as they all had expected when Ferula died.

"How are you feeling, my queen?" Zelaria asked, her brow furrowed with worry. Rhys had to stop himself from pursing his lips. She hadn't even sent a falcon last night. It was hard for him to reconcile that with the dramatic amount of worry Zelaria was showing at the moment.

"Better, thanks to Rhys." Medea held out her hand to him, and he took it, despite Tavyss growling softly at the contact. The dragon cleared his throat to hide his aggression.

"I must give credit where it's due. Your sister Circe was key in developing the antidote earlier this week. She's a brilliant alchemist and potion maker. The most talented witch I've ever known."

The muscles in Zelaria's face tightened. "Well, you can't have known many, Rhys." She laughed as if her words were a joke, but Rhys could hear the bitter jealousy in them.

"Where is my sister?" Medea asked.

"Home. She's due in later this morning." Rhys rested his hands in his pockets and thought about the night before, about the kiss. Had she dreamed of him the way he'd dreamed of her?

"Now, I must deliver the news, Medea," Zelaria said urgently. "We found the person who poisoned you."

Medea and Tavyss exchanged glances. "Who?" Tavyss asked.

"One of the staff. A man named Lazys. He was recently hired on by the house manager to fill a vacancy. We found a vial tainted with the poison in his chambers."

"I'll kill him," Tavyss growled.

"Fitting you do the deed, considering I believe he was here because of you," Zelaria said.

"What are you insinuating?" Medea leveled a sharp look at the witch.

"The man is a citizen of Paragon—a witch who grew up in Hobble Glen. I believe he's a spy."

Medea's brow furrowed. "A spy?"

Zelaria sighed and leaned back in her chair. "I warned you this would happen, Medea. Servants don't usually try to murder their employers without a motive. I couldn't get him to admit it, but I am sure he was sent by Paragon because you repeatedly refused their invitation. They don't trust you."

Rhys could hold his tongue no more. "Do you have any evidence linking this attack to the Obsidian Palace, Zelaria? Or are you assuming because he grew up in Paragon?"

She brushed her hands over her skirt. "I have no proof. When we caught him with the poison, he went completely mute. He refused to say a word, even when I threatened his life."

"Okay, then. What did it look like?" Rhys stared her down. He couldn't shake the feeling that Zelaria was spinning this tragedy to bolster her political motivations. He didn't care about relations with Paragon even half as much as he cared that there was a murderer out there who understood the properties of gila vine.

Zelaria turned. "Hmmm? The man is thin, brown hair, brown eyes."

"Not the man, the poison," Rhys pressed. "You said you caught him with the poison. What did it look like?"

Furrowing her brow as if the question put her out, she said, "A glass vial."

Rhys drew a container out of the inside pocket of his coat. "Like this one?"

She inhaled deeply. "Why, yes. Exactly like that."

Rhys frowned. The glass jars he used for samples weren't commonly used in homes. They were a tool of his trade, something only an experienced apothecary might have on hand. "What color was the poison inside?"

Zelaria cleared her throat. "I wasn't really paying attention to the color—"

"You were sure it was poison, though. How did you know it was poison if you didn't get a good look at it?"

She frowned and crossed her arms. "It smelled of anise. The same smell I'd noticed on Medea's glass. And now that I think about it, the liquid inside was clear."

"Clear? Are you sure?" Rhys asked.

"Of course I am! It must have been clear, or we would have seen it in her glass before the wine was poured."

Rhys slumped, shaking his head.

Medea sighed heavily. "What does it mean, Rhys? Why does it upset you that it was clear?"

"You were poisoned using a plant called gila vine. It grows on the border between Darnuith and Rogos and is native to the Mystic Wood. It has bright-green variegated leaves. If you boil it down into a tincture, it's usually green. A very good apothecary or wizard might be able to refine that tincture until it is clear, but it would take time and complex magic. Only an apothecary of some talent and experience would be capable of it."

Tavyss growled. "In other words, if the tincture was clear, someone more powerful than a common servant was involved. Someone with the power and resources to refine a deadly poison from a little-known plant."

Medea's hands went to her belly. "The servant had to be working for someone else."

"I'd bet on it." Rhys hated to be the bearer of bad news, but he was almost positive the man in the dungeon was a tool of someone far more dangerous.

"Precisely," Zelaria agreed, finger pointing toward the ceiling. "It all fits. The man is from Paragon, and the Paragonian royals would have the means to provide him with the poison. Medea, you simply must accept their invitation. This was a message. A warning. What you are doing, putting them off like this, is political positioning. They've assumed you're secretive and dangerous. Whether this man acted alone or not, I think it's clear *why* he acted."

Medea looked between Zelaria and Tavyss. "I'd like to question the man myself. Before we accuse the kingdom of Paragon of my attempted assassination, I think we should have more evidence."

Zelaria bowed her head. "As you wish, my queen. I've brought the carriage. We can return to the palace together."

"Not yet. I'd like to rest a bit longer. Thank you, Zelaria."

Zelaria stood slowly, leaning on her staff. "Are you certain, my queen? Your duties await."

"I'll be there soon." Medea dismissed Zelaria, and the adviser strode from the apothecary, looking as severe as when she'd walked in.

Once the door chimed and it was clear she was gone, Medea scrubbed her face with her hands. "Fates help us all. He might have killed any one of us if not for you and Circe."

Rhys pressed a hand to his chest. "It's our honor to be of service."

Medea licked her lips. "I wonder if the two of you might be of service once more."

Circe chose that moment to walk through the front door, the bell chiming above her head. She spotted Rhys through the door to the infirmary and hurried to him. "Is my sister okay?"

"She's fine," Rhys said.

But Tavyss's expression had turned stony. "Things are not fine. Zelaria believes Medea was targeted for assassination by Paragon."

Circe's jaw dropped in alarm, and Rhys curbed a strong desire to take her into his arms.

"We don't know that," Medea said. "Zelaria captured a servant who had the remains of the poison in his room. He hails from Paragon, and Zelaria assumes that means he's an assassin sent to kill me. But we have no proof the Obsidian Palace is behind this."

Tavyss sniffed. "I fear her assumptions are most likely correct."

Medea's head snapped around. "What are you saying, darling? You think your brother and sister are behind this?"

"Isolation has never worked for Darnuith," Tavyss said carefully. "Its witch queen needs to take her place as a leader of her kingdom. She must have a relationship with the rest of Ouros. I do think this was a warning and a threat. It's even possible Paragon already knows about me. If the servant sent a falcon to Eleanor and Brynhoff before he poisoned you—"

"We have to question this man. We have to know the truth before we can act." Medea scowled.

"I agree," Tavyss growled.

Rhys met Circe's gaze, but he had no answers for the questions in her eyes. "How can we help?" he asked.

Medea toyed with the gem around her neck, sending gold light dancing along the walls of the room. "I'm glad you asked. I was about to ask you for a favor, and I think you'll need Circe's help if you agree to it."

"What kind of a favor?" Rhys asked.

"I want you to make a truth serum. When we question this man Lazys, I want to know exactly who was pulling his strings."

Truth serum wasn't easy to make. Circe had never mixed such a complex potion, and to her chagrin, Rhys had no experience at the task either. But the apothecary's grimoire—inherited from his predecessor—contained the spell for one, and they perfected the potion on their third try.

Together, they escorted Medea and Tavyss into the dungeon, a vial of ruby-red liquid in Rhys's hand. The formula looked and smelled as the book described, but testing it was impossible. Without knowing what side effects the potion might have, they couldn't safely try it out on anyone they trusted, and anyone they didn't trust would not make for a valid test. But Circe's gut told her it was right and would work. She'd learned to trust her instincts when it came to potions.

Lazys was a rat of a man with a nose and chin that narrowed to a point and dark brown eyes that looked black in the shadows. His hair hung in stringy strands to his jaw. Slumped at the back of the cell, he seemed utterly worn down by his imprisonment, although the conditions in the dungeon weren't overly harsh. Circe noted the space was clean and the air was temperate. The man had clean water to drink.

"Lazys!" Tavyss yelled through the bars. "Are you ready to talk?"

"Fuck you," the man snapped.

The guards opened the cell and rushed in, seizing Lazys and tipping his head back. Rhys poured the potion into his mouth, and the guards held his mouth closed until he swallowed. When they released him, he thrashed against their hold. "Filthy bastards. Fucking vermin, all of you," he muttered.

Medea stepped to the bars. "Why did you try to poison me?"

The man gritted his teeth and writhed in his chair, his face turning red as he fought the compulsion to speak. Medea looked at her, and Circe held up her hand. "Give it a chance to work."

"You're unworthy!" the man blurted. "You don't belong here. You're mated to a traitor to Paragon. A witch mated to a dragon! Everyone knows what you're trying to do. First, you take Darnuith, then Paragon, then Ouros. Someone had to stop you."

"That isn't true," Medea argued, but the man refused to even look at her.

"Who sent you?" Tavyss growled.

The man shook his head, fighting the serum. "The true... and rightful... heir to the throne."

"Eleanor? Or Brynhoff?"

He shook his head. "They know what you've done,

traitor! They know who you are. I told them you were here. It's only a matter of time before they come for you."

Something wasn't adding up. Circe glanced at Rhys and saw the same questions in his eyes. "Where did you obtain the poison you put in the queen's glass?" Circe yelled.

The man grunted in pain, clamping his hands over his mouth. His face turned red, then purple.

"I think he's spelled not to answer," Rhys said, "The potion we gave him and the concealment spell are warring within him."

"Tell me!" Circe demanded. "Who?"

As if compelled by some unholy force, Lazys stood and ran at the wall at full speed, headfirst. His skull cracked against the stone, and he collapsed, unconscious, to the floor. Blood pooled near his head.

"Fuck!" Tavyss paced, wings outstretched as the guards rushed in and knelt beside the prisoner. Rhys pushed his way through, wand drawn, and placed his fingers on the man's neck.

"He's dead, my queen," Rhys said.

Circe couldn't suppress a gasp. "What kind of spell is strong enough to force a man to crush his own skull against the wall rather than give up a name?"

"One created by a powerful witch or wizard." Medea's scowl grew more pronounced as she watched the man's blood seep between the stones.

"One commissioned by my evil sister and half-wit brother," Tavyss said. "This is just wicked enough to be Eleanor's doing."

Medea turned to him, her face paling. "Tavyss, he implied they already know."

Tavyss shook his head. "Zelaria is right. We can't put it off any longer. We have to meet with them, Medea. If we don't, this man won't be the last they send for us. They will not stop until one of us is dead."

Circe saw the moment her sister came to terms with the truth. She shuddered.

Despite her obvious trepidation, Medea raised her chin defiantly and flattened her lips into a straight line. "If Eleanor wants to play, we play. We'll send a falcon today. It's time for Paragon to learn exactly who they are dealing with."

Circe knew that look. Medea had once faced the goddess Hera head on with that same look in her eyes. Her sister turned on her heel and strode toward the stairs, her spine ramrod straight. "It looks like the queen is going to punch back," she murmured to Rhys.

He slipped his hand into hers, and she clung to it desperately. "Fates watch over us all, I think she has to."

DAYS LATER, Circe found herself in a carriage rolling toward the Obsidian Palace. It shouldn't have been a surprise that Tavyss and Medea asked her and Rhys to come along. Someone from the Palace had tried to poison them. They might try again. Between the two of them, she and Rhys were the most likely to recognize another poisoning attack. Not to mention, Rhys could treat a number of ills caused by curses or evil enchantments. He carried a host of herbs, roots, and potions, including the antidote for gila vine poisoning, in his mobile apothecary basket.

They were cleared through the front gate by a serious-looking dragon in a red and black uniform and rolled through the front garden to the side entrance of the palace, where more uniformed guards escorted them inside. Circe couldn't help but gawk as they crossed a stunning veranda of solid obsidian that offered a stunning view of Hobble Glen and the Dark Mountains of Darnuith. Circe thought that if she squinted, she might see the Grimtwist Forest beyond the Sanguine River.

"Tavyss." A dark-eyed soldier in a uniform adorned with medals appeared before them. He gave a shallow bow, but the shadows in his eyes made Circe bristle. Whoever this man was, he did not want good things for Tavyss.

"Scoria," Tavyss said by way of greeting. "Is my sister in the dining room?"

Everyone here knew Tavyss, knew he was the eldest brother and the true heir. Yes, he'd abdicated his throne centuries ago to escape the obligations of his birth, but there was no question that Eleanor and Brynhoff would be far more comfortable with him dead. Circe felt in her sleeve for her wand, taking comfort in its presence as well as Rhys's big body by her side. He seemed to sense her unease and placed a supportive hand at the center of her back.

"I'll escort you to the dining room," Scoria said. "Eleanor and Brynhoff will join you in a moment. They've been called into an emergency meeting of the Council of Elders." Scoria led them into a massive room. At the center, a table constructed of a single slab of deep-red wood with an unusual zigzagging grain that was both exotic and beautiful waited for them. Opulent gold plates and jeweled goblets glinted in the light of silver candelabra. Candles flickered and cast soft light across the spread. Everything sparkled.

Circe had long understood that dragons were obsessed with treasure, and this dining room testified to that assumption. It was like standing aboard a pirate ship among stolen booty, a hodgepodge of gold, silver, and jeweled elements reflecting off the polished black stone walls. It overwhelmed the senses. She longed for something green, something alive.

At Scoria's behest, they sat and were left alone in the room.

"It's common for the king and queen of Paragon to listen in on their guests' conversations before they enter a room," Tavyss said quietly, although not so quiet that he was necessarily sure he couldn't be heard. Why hide it? He'd grown up here. He knew the way they played the game.

Rhys pulled out four small, clear crystals from his bag and dropped one into each of their hands. "For luck," he said.

Luck. Circe gave him a knowing smile. The crystals were enchanted to change color in the presence of poison.

The door at the back of the room opened, and a man announced, "Eleanor, Queen of Paragon."

A tall woman with a round face and silver eyes strode

into the room. Her purple dress billowed around her as if someone had frosted her in fabric.

"Hello, brother." She strode directly to Tavyss and gave him a stiff and awkward hug that made Circe's stomach clench. There was nothing warm in that embrace, and if Tavyss weren't a dragon, she'd have worried the queen might stab him when she pulled him close.

"Eleanor," Tavyss said. "And where is our brother?"

Eleanor threaded her fingers in front of her hips. "He can't make it. Paragonian business." She turned to Medea. "Finally, I am to meet the new queen of Darnuith." She extended her hand.

Even Circe knew that dragons didn't usually shake hands. Witches did. By Eleanor offering her hand, she was showing respect for their customs. Still, Circe had a bad feeling about this. It was disingenuous. She reminded herself that it was likely this woman who had attempted to kill her sister.

Medea shook Eleanor's hand tentatively. "I look forward to a positive relationship between our two kingdoms," she said flatly.

Eleanor gave a shallow bow and then took her place at the head of the table, where a servant pulled out a chair for her. "Unfortunately, the relationship between our kingdoms is already strained."

Circe's jaw clenched, but her sister never lost her cool.

"I was under the impression you invited us here for a peaceful meeting," Medea said. "If your intention isn't peace, perhaps Tavyss and I should leave." She rose from her chair.

"Sit down," Eleanor commanded. "I said the relationship was strained. Unless you wish to sour it completely, you will listen to what I have to say."

Tavyss pressed his dark bronze hands to the table, his chest rising and falling with his calming breaths. He turned fiery gold eyes on his sister. "What exactly is your complaint, sister?"

"You, Tavyss. You are the rightful heir to the kingdom of Paragon."

Circe swallowed hard. The food hadn't even been served yet and Eleanor was going straight for the jugular.

"I've told you time and time again, I've abdicated. I have no intention of ever ruling Paragon. The kingdom is yours and Brynhoff's." Tavyss balled his hands into fists on the table, face flushed with frustration.

Eleanor scoffed. "Oh, Tavyss." She shook her head. "You have always suffered under the delusion that you enjoy more freedom than you actually do." She snapped her fingers and pointed at her glass. A servant poured wine for her the color of blood. She lifted the glass and took a sip while the servant filled the rest of the glasses.

"I am free," Tavyss said. "I denounced my Paragonian citizenship. I am now a citizen of Darnuith."

Eleanor shook her head. "Dear, dear brother, you still don't understand. Villania always did coddle you. As did Falkon."

"What do Mother and Uncle have to do with this? They are no longer king and queen."

She held out her hand, and one of the uniformed

guards placed a scroll in it. "They now serve on the Council of Elders, and only hours ago, they confirmed the interpretation of the old law."

Tavyss's fists sprouted talons that dug into the wood table. "Old law?"

"You can't abdicate," Eleanor snapped. "Not for an opposing throne and not if you've already sired an heir to the kingdom."

Circe shook her head and stared at Medea. How did Eleanor even know about the baby? Had she heard correctly? Did this woman who had almost killed her, now suggest that her child had a claim to Paragon?

Tavyss's face paled. "Liar."

"Brynhoff and I had the council confirm only minutes ago." She handed the scroll to Tavyss. "An heir can abdicate provided he does not rule anywhere in the five kingdoms. It's obvious, if you think about it. It ensures against civil war. One brother cannot break from the royal family and found another kingdom. The law was written to account for younger heirs who might have their eyes set on acquiring a throne of their own, but it applies to you as well."

Medea scowled. "Then Tavyss hasn't broken the law. He is my consort, not king of Darnuith. He has no governing power. Darnuith is ruled only by its queen."

"Ah, but a little bird told me you are pregnant, Medea. A falcon, to be exact, from a sympathizer within your kingdom."

Circe exchanged glances with Rhys. So, it was true. Lazys had communicated everything to Paragon before his arrest. It had to have been Lazys. And the Council of

Elders knew about Tavyss and the baby. She felt sick. This was the worst-case scenario.

"Who told you this?" Tavyss growled, as if he didn't know about the man whom, only days ago, they'd watched bash his own head in.

"Don't deny it. I can hear the whelp's heartbeat." Eleanor's eyes narrowed on Medea's belly.

"I don't deny it." Tavyss's lips pulled back from his teeth. "I asked who the sympathizer was."

Eleanor ignored his request for a name. "The child in Medea's womb is the heir to Paragon." She turned her gaze on Circe, who ground her teeth, and then on Rhys. "As witches, you couldn't possibly understand how rare dragon children are. I may be queen, but I have not yet found a consort of my own. Even when I do, a successful pregnancy is never guaranteed among our kind. The old law is designed to ensure the throne is never left empty."

Medea scowled. "What exactly are you suggesting, Eleanor? Are you saying that you wish to cast off Brynhoff and take Tavyss as king?" She said it incredulously, like the very idea was ridiculous, but Circe saw the exact moment when she realized the truth of the matter.

Not a hint of humor colored Eleanor's expression when she answered. "That's exactly what I'm suggesting, Medea. Tavyss is the rightful king of Paragon, and he must do his duty or be put to death."

EIGHT

Throughout his life, Rhys had struggled to act in a crisis. He tended to overthink things, which left him hesitant and fraught with indecision. But it took no deliberation on his part to leap in front of Circe when Tavyss shot out of his chair and Eleanor sprang to her feet.

"Be careful what you wish for, Eleanor." Tavyss's dark wings stretched above his head, forming a wall of leathery flesh between Eleanor and Medea. From everything Rhys had heard about dragons and their mates, he had no desire to be in the vicinity of one whose protective instincts had been triggered. He glanced toward the exit and found an armed guard waiting there.

Circe slipped her hand into his.

"I don't waste my time on wishes, Tavyss," Eleanor said. "I am too focused on what could be. What *will* be. If you take the throne, Medea will be your consort, effectively uniting our kingdom with Darnuith. Your heir will be the next ruler of Paragon."

Medea got to her feet, wand drawn. "You'd force Tavyss into an impossible situation. Where would he live? Apart from me? By your side? Would you take my child from me too? Ruin our marriage, our mating? Cause us to fight each other if there is ever a political divide?"

"Lower your wand, witch, unless you'd like to pit it against dragon fire," Eleanor hissed, her voice gritty and raw. Rhys drew Circe closer to him when Eleanor's silver eyes flashed with light. That was her inner dragon coming to the surface.

Tavyss reached behind him and gently pushed Medea's wand aside, shaking his head. Smart move. None of them needed a war today or to be eaten by Eleanor's dragon if she shifted inside this room. Already, the temperature had risen several degrees. Sweat dripped from Rhys's temple.

"There must be another way to appease the old law, *sister*, that doesn't involve tearing my family apart." Tavyss said the word sister like it was a curse.

Eleanor raised her chin. "Simple. Medea must step down as queen of Darnuith and serve as your consort. She'll live here, in Paragon."

"How dare you suggest such a thing!" Circe snapped. "My sister was named queen by the Fates. You would offend the gods of Darnuith to appease the Goddess of the Mountain?"

Rhys squeezed her hand. "Careful," he warned. Eleanor's eyes were glowing again.

"I am told that queens have stepped down before," Eleanor said. "The Fates will name another. In Paragon, our goddess demands rule by blood. Not so in Darnuith. You or your healer might be chosen should your sister step down, and there would be no harm to your kingdom."

Circe looked as if she might crumple. She trembled in his arms, and a quick glance at Medea showed her visibly shaken as well. Rhys's blood began to boil. This wasn't a diplomatic dinner. It was an ambush. Eleanor might as well have punched all of them in the gut. Rhys could no longer bite his tongue.

"You've given our queen and consort a lot to think about, Eleanor, but as the queen's personal physician, I must demand you allow us to leave so that she can consider this matter in a less stressful environment. If she indeed carries the heir to Paragon, I think you'll agree she should be careful with her health."

Eleanor clasped her hands in front of her hips. "Very well, apothecary. Take your patient. I'd so looked forward to our dining together, but perhaps you're right. Tavyss and Medea do have a lot to think about."

Rhys had ushered Circe halfway toward the door when Eleanor addressed Tavyss again. "You have three days. Brynhoff and I have already shared your good news with the Council of Elders. They will expect your decision at their next gathering."

Talons sprang from Tavyss's knuckles, and a growl snapped from his throat. "Just tell me one thing, Eleanor. What does Brynhoff think of this plan you have to replace him with me? Does he realize he won't be king anymore if you succeed?"

She made a sound like a dark laugh, the corner of her

mouth curling. "Brynhoff will do as I tell him to do. Why do you suppose he's not here?"

Tavyss shook his head. "You'd sell out your own brothers for more power. This is low, even for you."

"Everything in life is about power." Eleanor's silver eyes took on the quality of frozen steel. "The sooner you realize that, Tavyss, the better off you will be. Power is far more important than wealth. All the riches in the world are useless if they can't be wielded to bend a knee or force a hand. Power transcends love. Love wanes. Love dies. Have you thought about what will happen to you if she dies?" Eleanor pointed her chin at Medea. "Love is a liability. It is meaningless. Long after her bones turn to dust, you will endure, and this mountain will likely outlive us both. Power is endurance. Power is strength. Power is eternity. And I plan to take it where I can get it."

"You're mad," Tavyss spat. Rhys had to agree. His skin was itching to get out of this room.

"Three days, Tavyss. Either you announce to the Council of Elders that you claim your right to the throne, or we come for Medea and the whelp."

Rhys was pressed against the door now, drenched in sweat from the mounting heat, Circe at his side. The door suddenly gave, and they spilled out into the hall. And then Tavyss and Medea were beside them. They rushed back to the carriage and fled toward Darnuith.

"Is it true?" Rhys asked once they were safely beyond the gates of the Obsidian Palace. "What she said about Paragonian law?"

Tavyss frowned. "Yes. I'd forgotten the old law, but the scroll she showed me was authentic. Seeing it triggered lessons from my youth. What she said is true. The pregnancy changes everything. I can abdicate the throne, but our child cannot. Medea is carrying the heir to Paragon. Eleanor's spies have confirmed the pregnancy, and she's shared both my identity and the existence of the baby with the Council of Elders. Paragon will not let this go. If I don't comply, they will attack Darnuith. They will do anything in their power to seize Medea and keep her in their custody until the heir is born."

"*Fuck.*" Medea punched the seat, her eyes brimming with tears. "That evil, manipulative worm!"

Rhys's heart pounded in his chest. He was a healer, not a warrior. He knew nothing of politics, but at the moment, he hated Eleanor more than he'd ever hated anyone. Nothing about it made sense to him. Old law or not, why would Eleanor want a reluctant co-regent? Why had she arranged to have Medea poisoned if the heir was so important to her and her people? It wasn't the right time to ask these questions, so he simply asked, "What will you do?"

"There's only one thing she *can* do," Circe said. Rhys turned his head to look at her and didn't recognize the woman he saw. Her eyes had filled with shadows, and her lips pulled back from her teeth in a sneer. "You need to use the book, Medea. You have unlimited power hanging around your neck. Show that bitch what happens when you mess with a Tanglewood sister."

EVER SINCE SHE'D come to Darnuith from the Garden of the Hesperides, Circe had wondered at how the witches here worshiped the Fates. The entire concept of the deities was that they controlled each person's future. With the right sacrifices and offerings, a witch could sway the gods to his or her side. She supposed it was terribly bad luck that she considered all the traditions around the Fates to be complete hooey. The events of her life had proven to her that if the Fates existed, they cared not about slaughtered lambs or offerings of fresh fruit. Based on her experience, the Fates loved chaos. They thrived on pain.

And what of Paragon's Goddess of the Mountain? Did the will of the Fates trump the will of Paragon's goddess? Who would win a war of the gods? For that matter, the goddess Circe was her namesake. The blood of the goddess ran in her veins and her sisters'. Didn't that give them the right and the power to challenge the law of any god?

Circe scoffed. "All I heard today was that according to some old law, the Goddess of the Mountain wants Tavyss and his child to rule Paragon. Well, the Fates chose Medea for the throne of Darnuith. I don't see any way to appease them both. That means you are justified, Medea. Use the book."

Rhys frowned. "Medea *could* renounce her throne. There is no law against it in Darnuith. The ritual of the Sacred Lots would happen again, and a new queen would be chosen."

Circe gasped. "That's vilt fodder! It's blackmail."

"Maybe there's another way," Tavyss said. He rested

his elbows on his knees and threaded his fingers at the knuckles.

Her sister got that look she did when she didn't like what was coming. Her lips pressed together, and her eyes tightened at the corners. "What way is that?"

"I can take back the throne and change the law."

The carriage turned eerily quiet. All eyes locked on Tavyss.

"If I become king, I will have the power to propose changes to the old law. Once I'm on the throne, I will make it so that Eleanor can lead Paragon unilaterally. Then I will return to Darnuith and to your side to serve as your consort."

Rhys stiffened, his eyes drifting to the window. "What happens when the baby is born?"

Tavyss's expression grew dark. "If I am no longer regent, then my son is no longer heir. I will make sure of it."

"If the Council of Elders passes such a change," Circe added skeptically. Hate surged in her veins like acid. She was furious on her sister's behalf. What had happened today was nothing short of cruel.

"It's the most peaceful solution," Tavyss said.

"Fuck peace," Circe snapped. "Use the book and make the old law go up in flames. You have the power of the gods around your neck. Flatten Paragon to the ground if you have to. Use it."

Beside her, Rhys stared speechless in her direction. He didn't know. He didn't understand what they could do.

Medea met her gaze and held it. Her eyes burned

with fierce blue fire. Eleanor underestimated them. The bond between her and her sister thrummed, and Circe had no doubt that somewhere in Darnuith, Isis could feel it too. She reached across the space and took her sister's hand.

Nothing more was said. Nothing more needed to be.

NINE

"Come in. I'll fix you something to eat," Circe opened the door wider for Rhys when they arrived at her cottage. He still looked overwhelmed by what had happened in Paragon. He stood in the doorway, staring at her as the carriage pulled away. "Isis is still out. Probably hunting with Brody. Their hunting party sometimes spends the night on the ice ridge. The elderbeasts are easier to take down at daybreak."

She should have been starving considering they hadn't had a single bite to eat or drink in Paragon, but her stomach was too busy tying itself in knots for hunger to set in. She was relieved when he followed her inside. The thought of being alone right now made her shudder.

"You're in luck. I had a delivery from the market just yesterday. I'll fix us something."

He nodded. "We should eat."

She grinned at him. "I'm still getting used to the local ingredients, but I think you'll enjoy it." She pulled some cubed elderbeast out of the icebox, along with an assortment of roots and vegetables, and tossed it into her cauldron. Shoving a log into the belly of the stove, she used her wand to ignite it and swung the pot over the fire.

"Can I help with something?" Rhys asked softly.

"No." She smiled at him, casting a spell into the cauldron to accelerate the cooking. "It practically cooks itself. Wine?"

He took a seat at the table. "Please."

"Do you want to know what kind I have?"

"Doesn't matter. After tonight, I'll drink anything." He stared at the ceiling, looking miserable.

She popped a cork and poured a glass of deep red. "What's bothering you? I sense it's more than just what happened in Paragon. You bristled when Tavyss suggested trying to change the law." She handed him the glass.

He sighed. "I'm a simple man, Circe. A healer and apothecary. I don't know anything about politics."

"But?"

"But I don't think Tavyss appreciates how bad it would look for him to become king then return here to rule by Medea's side. Darnuith has always been ruled by a single monarch. Even if he calls himself her consort, it will be viewed by the people of Darnuith as if she is a sock puppet for Paragon. They'll never accept it."

She sighed. "I never thought of it that way."

"I'm afraid the only thing Medea can do to avoid war with Paragon is to step down."

"Or put on a show of force so powerful Eleanor, Brynhoff, and the Council of Elders have no choice but to change the law themselves."

Rhys sipped the wine she'd poured for him, looking contemplative. "You said she had a book powerful enough to do so. What did you mean by that?"

No one had ever sworn Circe to secrecy about the golden grimoire, but she hesitated. It was never a good idea to flaunt power. She'd only mentioned the book in the carriage because she trusted Rhys. The fact that Medea and Tavyss hadn't corrected her or made any indication they wanted her to keep it a secret from Rhys meant they trusted him too. Still, how could she explain it without scaring him away?

"I've told you before that my sisters and I were born in the Garden of the Hesperides, Hera's garden."

"Yes."

"Our father is a descendant of the sorceress Medea, and our mother is a descendant of the goddess Circe."

He choked on his wine. "Sorry. Did you just say you are the descendant of an actual goddess?"

Circe nodded. "When we became young adults, we quickly exhausted the magical knowledge of our parents, and so we cast a spell to conjure a more powerful teacher, specifically a book that could teach us what they could not. We conjured Hera's golden grimoire."

This time, Rhys carefully placed his glass down, the liquid in its belly rippling until he pulled his trembling hand away. He kept his face carefully impassive, but his voice was strained when he asked, "Hera, as in the queen of the gods?"

Circe nodded. "That's why we came here. Hera can't set foot on Ouros thanks to an ancient celestial law. The book is ours. It came to us. We earned it."

His throat bobbed on a swallow. "Where is this book now?"

"Medea wears it around her neck. We spelled it into a diamond she had mounted on a chain so that she could carry it with her always."

His eyes narrowed. "I thought its glow was exceptional."

"That's because it holds the power to flatten Paragon's mountain to dust." Circe scoffed and crossed her arms. "So, you see, there is no need for Medea to bow to anyone. She's been kind thus far, reluctant to exercise the full power at her disposal. But now they've pushed us too far. She needs to retaliate."

His face fell. "But people would die."

"Paragonians will die because of their cruel and heartless queen."

Rhys's eyes narrowed, and the look of disappointment on his face cut to the bone. "You can't mean that. They're innocent, Circe. They didn't choose Eleanor. She claimed the throne by blood."

Circe sipped her drink. "I'm so sick of my sister being shoved around. It's not fair what they are doing to her, Rhys."

He picked up his glass and tossed back the rest of the wine. "Life isn't fair. It wasn't fair that my wife died of a fever that I would learn to cure five years after her death. It isn't fair that the citizens of Darnuith trust my apothecary less since I've hired you and speak quite openly about it behind both of our backs."

"Rhys..." She tipped her head and sighed.

"It's not fair that I will never fire you, even if all my

patients leave me and I am at risk of starving to death, because every time I see you, it's as if the sun has finally risen and conquered the dark night of my heart."

"I feel that way too."

He stood and headed toward the door.

"Wait. Where are you going?"

"To think about the fact that the woman whose caring and empathetic nature, the healer who is my friend and almost more, would rather her sister use celestial power to flatten an entire kingdom than step down from a role she didn't choose for herself in the first place." His voice cracked as he said it, and she thought he looked older then. Worn.

She stood. "Rhys!" He turned back to her, nothing but a silhouette in her doorway. "Come back. What about dinner?"

He gave her a shallow smile. "I've lost my appetite."

He slipped into the night, and the door closed behind him.

"I HOPE I'm not interrupting anything." Circe could tell by the bags under her sister's eyes that she hadn't slept well. Still, Medea smiled as she always did when she saw her and guided her to a comfortable chaise in the palace salon.

"What brings you here so early this morning? Is everything okay?" It was like Medea to be concerned for everyone else's comfort when it was her world falling apart.

"It's fine. I just... I've been thinking over what I said yesterday in the carriage about using the book to go to war with Paragon."

Medea sat and folded her hands in her lap as a servant poured them both a cup of tea. "Would you please excuse us?" she asked the servants. A few moments later, the sisters were alone in the room. "It was a valid idea and an option Tavyss and I are considering. Eleanor wants Tavyss to take the throne, which means she wants to try to use him to advance her position. All she understands is power. If he bends to her will, I know in my heart we'll regret it. She will continue to take and take and manipulate him, us, and our child for as long as we live. You can see it in her eyes. There will be no end to her cruelty."

Circe chewed her lip. That was, in fact, why she'd brought up the idea in the first place. She'd thought the same thing. But Rhys was right, and she had to get what she came to say off her chest. "It's just, last night, Rhys helped me to understand that the people of Paragon don't get to choose their ruler. Most Paragonians are innocent. If you use the book, I think you should wield its magic in the palace against Eleanor and Brynhoff. Limit casualties."

"Kill the dragon within its den, instead of bringing down the entire mountain with her in it."

"Yes." Circe sipped her tea.

"I know you, sister. I know you never meant for me to level their kingdom, even if I could muster the power it would take to do it."

Circe stared at her hands, disappointed in herself.

"Then you don't know me as well as you think you do. When I saw how Eleanor treated you, I wanted her to die. I wanted all of them to die."

Medea smiled. "Do you mean to tell me that my dear sister, who always follows the rules and used to tell on herself to our parents when we were children, has developed a murderous streak?"

Although her sister laughed, Circe saw the darkness within her heart. It was there in a separate, closed-off part of herself, and it scared her that it seemed to be growing. "I'm tired, Medea. I'm tired of the people of Darnuith threatening us. Even the ones who feign politeness are achingly distant. I'm tired of missing Mom and Dad and knowing we can never visit them again without putting them or us at risk. I'm tired of being pushed around by everyone and everything, or constantly moving and changing to give everyone else space and not taking any for myself. It's like I'm supposed to float around, a benevolent ghost who's good enough to help where help is needed but not good enough to invite into anyone's life."

A groan escaped Medea's throat. "Why is it that I feel our discussion has taken an abrupt turn from my strategy addressing Paragon to your personal life, Circe?"

Circe sighed. "Because it has. I think I've fallen in love with Rhys."

Medea's brow arched. "I'd wondered. He does look at you as if you are single-handedly responsible for all the stars in the heavens."

With a scoff, Circe brought her cup to her lips. "Honestly, I think he's wise to keep me at a distance.

People don't trust us here. Why should he take the risk?"

"Circe Tanglewood, stop it. Stop it right now. He'd take the risk because you're worth it, and if he doesn't, he can't be worth the price of your affection. You're beautiful and powerful. If people here still don't trust us, maybe that's a sign that we've already accomplished whatever plan the Fates had for us when they chose me." Medea played with the edge of her dress.

"What does that mean? You can't be seriously considering stepping down."

She nodded. "I am. I never needed to be queen. All I ever wanted was to have the freedom to exercise my magic and to love Tavyss in peace. All of this just fell into my lap, and with the baby coming... I wouldn't be disappointed to simply be his consort."

Circe leaned back in her chair. Her sister shouldn't have to bow to anyone, but if she wanted something different for her life, Circe would be there to support her. "I'm here for you, always. You know that, don't you?"

"Of course I do. Sisters are forever."

TEN

Glass shattered around Rhys's feet. Fuck if the specimen jar hadn't slipped from his fingers. Or had he thrown it? He'd felt like throwing it. Felt like hurling it at the closest wall. All he could think about was Circe. Her face when he'd left her cottage would be seared into his brain until the day he died.

He'd been unfair to her, a fucking bastard saying what he had. Anyone would contemplate violence after the encounter they'd had with Eleanor, especially when the person being threatened was one's sister. It was only natural for Circe to suggest such a thing.

He grabbed a dustpan and started sweeping up the broken glass. Who was he kidding? He'd pushed her away on purpose. The notion of attacking Paragon was a handy excuse to extricate himself from a situation where he was getting too close. He wanted her. He'd wanted her for weeks now. Thoughts of Circe had monopolized his days and heated his nights.

And acting on that desire felt like a terrible sin. Was

their kiss a betrayal of June? Despite her being dead, he'd never thought he'd love another. Entering into a relationship with Circe meant throwing his carefully ordered life to the wind, breaking down all the walls he'd put in place to protect himself and opening himself to a woman whose power should threaten him and whose very presence was unsettling to many.

The bell rang, and he emptied the dustpan into the trash before making his way to the counter. Emily Wraithwing. He'd helped her with a skin condition she was suffering from earlier in the month. "Good morning, Emily."

"To you too, Rhys. I always pray to the Fates to watch over you."

"What brings you back in today? Didn't the salve work?"

"It did. But I saw that Circe's broom was gone from the broom keep and took a chance you'd be alone. I thought we could talk." The tiny, wrinkled woman hooked a finger under her chin.

"What's on your mind?"

"It's just, the other witches and I, we're worried about you, Rhys. It's hard to believe that June would have wanted this for you."

"Wanted what for me?"

She cleared her throat. "Well, you know, you're working so closely with Circe."

"Circe is an extremely talented healer, Emily. We're all lucky to have her."

"Talented, yes. When the three sisters first came to Darnuith, we were all delighted with their contributions.

But you must admit that she and her sisters are strange. They've never truly been a part of this community."

"Only because they're not from here. Circe and her sisters have been nothing but good for Mistcraven. The Fates chose Medea for a reason, Circe has helped me here more than I can say, and everyone has been enjoying the bountiful results of Isis's hunting since she arrived."

Emily snorted. "A woman hunting. Strange, I tell you. All three are strange, and the queen mated to a dragon!" She narrowed her eyes. "It makes one wonder if there wasn't some nefarious purpose to their arrival. With magic like theirs, it wouldn't be impossible to tamper with the Sacred Lots."

"No one has ever been able to tamper with the Sacred Lots before. It's ancient magic. And Medea had no access to the stones."

The elderly woman made a sound deep in her throat. "Even you must recognize how odd a choice it was, Rhys. My heart breaks for Zelaria. She should have been chosen. The queen's adviser is always chosen. It doesn't make any sense."

His gaze swiveled toward the ceiling. "Circe is a good person. For Fates' sake, she made the salve that healed you." Emily's eyes grew large at that revelation. "I'm not going to speculate why the Fates didn't choose Zelaria, but they didn't. It's been months. Medea has proven herself a fine queen. Even if you don't agree with it, at least respect the choice the Sacred Lots made for us."

She shook her head. "I'm sorry, Rhys. I know you're a good man, but I think you're wrong to trust them, and

I'm afraid for you. I think Circe might have you under her spell. I'm taking my business to Shadowvale's."

Rhys was left speechless as the old woman turned on her heel and strode out the door. Only seconds later, the door opened again, and Circe strode in, leaving her broom in the broom keep just outside the door. "Was that Emily I saw speeding for home? Didn't the salve work?"

"Worked like a charm."

"Then why did she look like she was trying to swallow her face?"

All Rhys wanted to do was dig in his apothecary for some mystic snail shell and spend the rest of the day in a hammock watching rainbows shoot across the sky. He couldn't fathom telling Circe what he'd just heard, and he wasn't ready to face the disagreement he'd had with her the night before. Just once, he wanted things to be easy, certain, uncomplicated. Why did he have to be falling in love with Circe, whose enigmatic past and strange powers could cost him his business and maybe his life if he wasn't careful?

He rubbed his face, catching the thought as it floated through his spinning head. The answer was there in the question, wasn't it?

"Rhys?"

"She's switching to Shadowvale's apothecary."

"What? Why?"

"Because she found out you made the salve, and she doesn't trust you or your sisters."

"I could have told you she doesn't trust me. How did she find out that I made it?"

"I told her."

Circe huffed, extending her hands toward him, palms up in utter exasperation. "Why would you do such a thing?"

"Because it's unfair how she treats you. You and your sisters. You're a powerful healer, and she needs to show some respect."

"But, Rhys... You'll lose your business. You don't owe me credit. You don't owe me anything! Maybe I should quit. If I left, your patients would return in time."

"Fuck that. I don't want you to leave. Don't let them do that to you, Circe. Those harpies have cursed, wagging tongues and don't deserve a second of your attention."

He couldn't stand the tension in the room, the disappointment that clung to her as she tried to process Emily's attitude toward her. He wanted to take her in his arms, to soothe her, but after the way he'd stormed out the night before, it didn't seem appropriate. He turned his attention to straightening the counter, just to dull the edges of the intensity between them.

"I thought after last night you'd jump at the chance to be rid of me." He lifted his gaze to hers, the arresting blue drawing him in again.

"No," he said softly. He knew it was a curt answer. Maybe he owed her more. Maybe the less he said, the better. The air around her seemed to buzz with her power—or was that some kind of magnetism? He desperately wanted to touch her and kiss away the pain he saw in her eyes.

"But... you were right. I went to see Medea this morning... That's why I was late. I told her what you told me about the people of Paragon being innocent. She never actually intended to turn Eleanor's kingdom into a wasteland, but our conversation definitely made her understand what kind of situation we're in."

His heart felt as if it was sliding along his rib cage, melting like butter in a frying pan. "You visited your sister this morning... because of me?"

She rounded the counter and took a step toward him. "Yes. You were right, Rhys. What I said last night, I said out of anger and frustration. It's not just Eleanor. It's Emily and people like her. Last night, all I could think about was wanting Medea to stand up for us after how Eleanor treated her, but I'm glad you said what you said. It reminded me that there are innocent people out there. If we lose our ability to know right from wrong, we're no better than Eleanor is."

Rhys watched her, stunned by her goodness. How was it the others couldn't see how decent she was down to her soul?

"So, are we good, Rhys?"

He cleared the thickness from his throat. "We were always good."

Her eyes glinted, wet in the light. "Thank the Fates. I couldn't bear losing you. You're my only friend in Darnuith."

"I'm not your friend," he said absently.

She jolted back as if he'd struck her.

He held up a hand. "That didn't come out right. I don't want to be your friend," he said softly, moving closer. He didn't stop until he was close enough to feel the heat from her body and smell the winter air on her skin. "I want to be more than your friend."

He brushed his lips lightly over hers.

"Oh," Circe said, the word a hard breath in her throat. "I don't want to be your friend either."

ELEVEN

Circe knew this was hard for him as Rhys's lips brushed hers in invitation. He wanted her, that was clear enough, but his emotions were complicated. She felt reluctance in the tension of his shoulders, likely guilt over his deceased wife, maybe even a sense of danger over what was happening with her sister, and no doubt apprehension regarding what he was doing to his business and only source of income. He'd done so much for her. She needed to do right by him.

"I don't want to complicate things for you," she said.

He drew his wand and pointed it at the door.

"Who's there?" she asked, thinking he must be protecting her from whatever might come through it.

With a twirl of his wrist, the sign in the window flipped from open to closed, the lock slid into place, and the curtains shut over the windows. He looked at her hungrily, lips drawn into a wolfish grin, lids heavy. The danger wasn't out there. It was in here.

"I don't want you to do anything you'll regret," she

warned. "It's okay if you want to take it slow or wait to see what happens with the queen."

"Right now, I'm not thinking about the queen," he said softly.

"But what about Emily and the store?"

"I'm not thinking about that either." His gaze was positively feral.

She lowered her chin. "What about June?"

In answer, he reached out and grabbed a fistful of her hair, tugging her flat against his chest. She allowed herself to mold to him, her body opening at the feel of hard muscle under his tunic. His mouth crashed down onto hers, and there was no question in his kiss now, only an insistent, claiming desire.

Circe welcomed it, opened wider to let him in, her hands feeling along his rib cage to his back. She fisted his shirt, stroking his tongue with her own. Teeth clashed. His fist tightened in her hair just to the point of pain. This was no gentle kiss. This was desperate. Wanting. Needing.

He spun her around, pressed her back against the wall. Clasping her wrists in one hand, he lifted them above her head. She arched into him. His palm skimmed up her side and squeezed her breast, kneading it through her dress.

She'd grown used to the way Rhys ordered her about the apothecary. It shouldn't have surprised her that he kissed the same way. Every touch was a command. Like always, she was more than willing to submit. She softened in his arms.

Fates, she was wet with need. She wanted him rough

and hard inside her, filling her. For someone who always followed the rules, Circe wanted desperately to break them all today.

She gasped when he pinched her nipple, and he captured her breath in his mouth, kissed her again like his life depended on it, like he was breathing the air from her lungs. His fingers danced down the front of her dress, undoing the buttons there. Rough fingers slipped inside, skin-to-skin, and massaged her breast again.

"I love that your nipples are hard for me." His breath was hot against the shell of her ear. He trailed his lips along her pulse, over her collarbone, and lower to flick hot and wet across the tip of her nipple. Cool air chilled the wet trail he left behind. Desire shot like sparks through her blood.

"Oh Fates, Rhys—"

He dropped her hands and pushed the dress off her shoulders along with her chemise. The material pooled around her ankles. He stepped back, a low groan coming from his throat as he took in her naked body. She toed off her shoes.

He came at her like a dark wind, grabbing her waist and lifting. Her bottom landed on the counter. "Oh," she said, the word formed from both surprise and breathlessness. His intensity was like a brand against her skin. Everywhere he touched burned.

Guiding her back against her elbows, he smoothed his fingers between her breasts. His lips were on her belly, kissing her navel. Lower. The edge of his short beard grazed her inner thigh. He might as well have struck a match. She burned. Every inch of her. She was going up in flames.

She gasped when he kissed her at her center, his lips pressing against her most sensitive flesh.

"Rhys…"

He licked up her folds, sending pulses of lightning branching through her veins. So much pleasure. So much need. He played her body like an instrument, and it sang for him. Head thrown back, she wrapped her thighs around his shoulders and rode his mouth. He didn't disappoint. His tongue worked her toward a sharp edge, and she dove over it, the orgasm ricocheting through her like pure unadulterated magic.

When she could see again, she glanced between her thighs and saw he was still completely dressed. How could he look so cool and collected when she'd just been reduced to a rippling pool of pleasure on his counter? This wouldn't do. She reached for him, but he backed away, lifting his tunic over his head himself.

That carnal, wolfish grin was back, and something else. Magic darkened his eyes, made his skin golden with its power. The air was thick with it. Not just his but hers. It tangled around them like a gathering storm.

His pants were gone, and she chewed her lip as she watched him. He was hard and thick, and she needed him, needed him thrusting inside her. Needed him to be hers in every possible way.

"As much as I'd like to take you right there, I don't think this old counter can withstand what I plan to do to you." He wrapped her legs around his hips and her arms around his neck. "Hang on."

On strong legs, he carried her up the stairs at the back of the apothecary, his hands supporting her by the thighs as if she weighed nothing. She'd never been in his private residence before, but she only saw a glimpse of red and black before his lips were on hers again and her back slapped against a mattress.

"This isn't going to be gentle." The blunt head of his cock pressed against her opening.

She opened her mouth to say she didn't want him to be gentle. She wanted it hard and fast. But the words never had a chance to leave her mouth. He thrust into her slick heat, and she almost came undone again at the pressure, the way he filled every inch of her.

And then he was over her, thrusting between her thighs. Rough and deep. She arched again as intense pleasure tore through her. Overwhelmed her. Hovering on the edge of pain. An impassioned sound somewhere between a scream and a moan tore from her throat.

Rhys was right there with her, tipping over the edge into oblivion with one final thrust, filling her with wet heat.

Through the aftershocks, her mind was vaguely aware that more than sex was happening between them. Magic gathered in the room like morning mist. Her pulse beat in time with his, tiny sparks dancing between their bodies. Still buried in her, he threaded his fingers with hers and brought his lips to her ear.

"There will be no more talk of leaving here. Not to spare me from whispers or from violence. I want you with me, Circe. Always. Do you understand?"

She pressed the side of her face to his, breathing him

in. He smelled of gathered herbs and crisp mountain air. "Agreed."

Shifting to his side, he pulled her against his chest. "Good."

She drifted off, perfectly content for the first time in as long as she could remember.

THREE HEAVY THUMPS WOKE CIRCE, her lids flying open in alarm. Rhys was already propped on one elbow, staring toward the door, brow furrowed. "Someone's knocking, downstairs."

"You'd better go. Maybe it's an emergency." He did run an apothecary after all. Someone might be sick or injured.

"Why wouldn't they go to Shadowvale's? The sign clearly says we're closed." The pounding came again, more urgently.

Circe kissed his jaw. "Probably because it's an emergency."

A gusty sigh left his lungs, and he reluctantly climbed out of bed. Cold moved in. She pulled the blanket more tightly around her.

"Barely a customer in weeks, and the one time I plan to spend three days in bed, suddenly someone needs help," he grumbled.

She laughed at the disgruntled look he gave her. "Three days?"

He shot her a wink as he dressed hastily in breeches and a tunic from a polished redwood wardrobe in the corner of the room. He swept back in and pressed a kiss to her mouth. "Don't move. I'm not done with you."

She gave him a wicked grin and watched him jog from the apartment and down to the apothecary below. Once he was gone, she lifted the blanket and stared down at herself, at the body she hadn't known was capable of so much pleasure. Her smile broadened until she could feel it in her ears.

The chatter of raised voices came through the floor, and then she heard footsteps on the stairs. Rhys marched back into the room, her dress in his hands. He handed it to her, his face flushed. "Er, your sister is downstairs. She wants to talk to us both. Says it's important."

Circe shook her head, confused. "Isis?"

"No. The queen, Medea. I think it's serious. And Circe, she knows you are up here. Your dress was on the floor. Please dress quickly and assuage her fears that I've done something horrid to you. I'd love not to spend time in the dungeon."

Circe dressed quickly and hurried down to the main floor of the apothecary. Medea waited near the door in a purple dress that flowed gracefully from her shoulders. Circe rushed to her and pulled her into her arms.

"Medea, what's going on?" Circe felt a strain along their sisterly bond and could see Medea had been crying. She'd stationed her guards outside the door. That was rare. Whatever it was Medea had come to tell her must be sensitive indeed.

"I'm sorry, Circe. Truly." Her eyes flicked to Rhys and then to her mussed hair. "I can see I'm interrupting something. If it weren't important—"

"Stop. You are welcome any time. Please, tell me what has happened!"

"Tavyss has decided. We sent a falcon to Paragon. He's challenging Brynhoff for the throne. Once he's installed as king of Paragon, I will step down as queen of Darnuith."

"Fates, Medea, are you sure?"

She took a deep breath and let it out slowly. "I am. This is best for everyone. Please keep it confidential, though, until all is settled. I don't plan to lay my cards on the table until the last second, in case Eleanor has tricks up her sleeve. I haven't even told Zelaria of my plans. Not until Tavyss's rule is imminent."

Circe glanced at Rhys. "You can count on us. We won't say a word."

Beside her, Rhys nodded. "Whatever you need. We're here for you."

Medea's chin dropped. "I'm glad you said that, Rhys, because I have a favor to ask. In fact, that's why I'm here."

Medea wasn't keen on asking for favors. On the contrary, she was normally a pillar of independence. "What's happened, sister?"

"After we sent the falcon to Paragon, we received one back. Eleanor has called a special session of the Council of Elders to discuss Tavyss's decision. Tavyss must state his intent to them in person, and they must formally accept his challenge to the throne. If all goes well, his coronation date will be announced in two nights' time."

"You're going back to Paragon tomorrow?" A chill

caused Circe to hug herself. Eleanor's cruel ways still lingered fresh in her mind.

"We are."

"Do you want us to accompany you again?"

She shook her head. "I have reason to believe that Eleanor wants this meeting to happen a bit too much. Her enthusiasm unsettles me." She pulled a roll of parchment from her bag and handed it to Circe.

"The *Daily Dragon?*" Circe read aloud from the newspaper. "The Eyes and Ears of Paragon." Her eyes skimmed the headline article. "Return of Royalty: Heir Apparent Plans to Challenge Brynhoff for the Throne."

"Look at the date," Medea said.

"This morning." Circe frowned. "Before you sent your falcon?"

Medea nodded. "Eleanor must have leaked this to their press. Very few knew Tavyss's identity before yesterday. This was an attempt to force his hand. If he hadn't intended to challenge Brynhoff, this article would have been enough to send rumors flying all over Ouros. Eleanor is orchestrating every move we make, and I just don't trust her."

Rhys scoffed, reading over Circe's shoulder. "I don't either. This isn't just manipulative. She's gained control of the narrative. This makes it sound as if Tavyss is the one demanding his place in the kingdom and threatening violence if he doesn't get his way. Ironic, considering the truth. Eleanor invited—no, forced his decision using the old law. She said the Council of Elders agreed with her interpretation of that law. None of that is even in this article. This makes it sound like you're behind this, Medea, as if you want it to gain political power."

"Yes. But there's more." She sighed. "I'm concerned that someone in Darnuith is working with her."

"What? Who?" Circe bristled.

Medea held up a hand. "It's a theory, really. It just doesn't add up why Lazys attempted to kill me if what Eleanor wanted was for Tavyss to rule by her side. She knew I was pregnant. How long had she known? And she knew that Tavyss was the former heir apparent to Paragon, despite our efforts to keep his identity secret. She knew all this long before we arrived in Paragon. There was no surprise on her face. She'd already discussed his existence with the Council of Elders. She's known all this time. Which means someone from Darnuith is in league with her."

"I thought we already knew it was Lazys," Circe said. "Eleanor must have cursed him to do her will."

"Maybe." She sighed. "But again, then why poison me? And, as Rhys questioned before, who made the poison? Dragons are not adept at such things. Although Eleanor likely has a witch in her employ, it's such a strange move given her next one."

"I agree," Rhys said. "The choice of poison suggests someone with in-depth knowledge of the flora of Rogos. There's no way Lazys refined it. Someone gave it to him to give to you and cursed him to kill himself rather than give up the true perpetrator."

Medea nodded. "Which is why, this time, I need you two and Isis to stay here. Keep your eyes open. We've told no one our plans. With your ears to the ground, perhaps you can learn who in Darnuith wants us dead."

"I worry about you," Circe said. "It's not safe for you and Tavyss to go alone. What if you are poisoned again?"

Medea ran a hand over the small mound of her stomach. "There are benefits to being mated to a dragon. Last night, Tavyss fed me his tooth."

"His *tooth.*" Circe bristled. "Why?"

"Dragon's teeth hold magical properties. He's bound this body to his immortality. I can't be killed as long as he lives. It's a dragon's oldest and strongest inherent magic. Aside from beheading, I can't be killed."

Circe exchanged looks with Rhys. "Are you sure about this magic?"

Medea drew her wand from her sleeve and, with a whispered incantation, dragged it across her hand. A deep cut parted her skin. Circe watched the blood pool in her palm. But then, like a miracle, the wound started to heal. She stared in wonder as the blood was drawn back inside, the skin knitting together, bright pink, then silver, then as if the cut had never happened.

"Fates' fury," Rhys mumbled. Circe exchanged glances with him. She'd never seen anything like this.

"So, will you help me? Will you be my spies in Darnuith while I'm away?" Medea asked.

"Of course. We'll get to the bottom of this, Medea."

She nodded. "I hope so. Because I fear the person who tried to murder me and my son still walks among us, and soon I will not be in a position to bring them to justice."

TWELVE

After Medea and Tavyss had left for Paragon, Rhys and Circe had agreed to divide and conquer. While Circe watched his apothecary, Rhys planned to visit Viktor Franwise and find out if anyone else had access to the gila vine on his property. When he returned, Circe would go to the market and listen for wagging tongues that might give them clues as to who was behind Medea's poisoning.

Rhys landed his broom at the edge of Viktor Franwise's property. He was a good mile from the front door of the man's farmhouse, but it was never a good idea to fly over another witch's sheep. Doing so was practically asking to be hit with a petrification spell.

He started up the drive toward the red farmhouse on foot. The air around him thickened as he drew near, and Viktor materialized in front of him, a smile spreading across his graying features when he saw who had set off his wards.

"Ah, Rhys. Tell me you have good news. I lost another sheep last night to the ivy!"

Rhys held up his apothecary basket. "Have it here, my friend. Enough antidote for you to cure half your herd if you needed to, along with a tonic that should keep the growth at bay."

The elderly man whooped and thumped Rhys on the back. "I knew you and Circe could do it. If you don't mind hearing it, people told me not to trust Bloodgood's with a Tanglewood sister working there, but they don't know a damn thing! Ya ask me, if the sisters are so powerful, it would do a body good to have them on our side."

Rhys smiled warmly. "Circe is powerful and clever, but also the kindest person I know."

Viktor studied his face for a moment, and Rhys wondered if he'd laid it on a bit thick. Could Viktor see the love he felt for Circe in his eyes?

"Well, come in. Pern will want to ply you with tea and biscuits before you go. She'll be so happy to hear you've found a cure."

Rhys followed the man into the big red farmhouse and was greeted with a hug by Viktor's wife before she knew a single thing about what he had in his bag. The elderly woman's ample frame engulfed him in the same back-thumping embrace her husband had delivered. He was promptly whisked into the kitchen, where tea and treats were already waiting.

"Did you solve the ivy problem?" she asked as she poured.

"I did."

"Fates alive, Viktor, you were right about this one!" She loaded a plate for him.

Rhys wasted no time pulling the vials of antidote and several large jars of the ivy deterrent from his bag. Viktor left the room for a few long moments and returned with a thick envelope. "We'd agreed on a fee for the antidote. I doubled it in light of the tonic to keep the ivy at bay. Sound fair to you?"

Rhys nodded, a sense of relief flooding him. He'd been willing to simply give Viktor the tonic, considering how dangerous the ivy was. Double his usual fee for custom spellwork meant he'd be set financially for the rest of the season. Right now, when business was slow and a new relationship with Circe meant it was about to get slower, the money was enough to save his hide.

"More than fair. Thank you for your business." He reached out and shook Viktor's hand. He tucked the envelope inside his jacket, then took a bite of one of Pern's biscuits. While he chewed, he wondered the best way to ask about the ivy without sounding nosy and intrusive. *Has anyone else visited your farm recently?* seemed far too forward and might raise untoward alarm.

Pern smiled at him over her teacup. "Should I send a falcon to Zelaria to let her know you've come by, or will you tell her?"

He lowered the rest of the biscuit to his plate. "Why would you need to tell Zelaria that I've come by?"

"Oh, weren't you both working together on the cure? She was here before, right after you were. She took samples of the ivy."

"Zelaria took samples of gila vine? When?" Rhys had

to force himself to swallow what was in his mouth, because his appetite had been replaced by a rush of nausea.

Pern nodded. "Right after you did. Over a cycle ago. Maybe she was working on the problem independently. I should send her a falcon to let her know it's taken care of."

"No," Rhys said quickly, ice forming in his gut. "I'll tell her myself. I'd like to tell Zelaria what I've learned." Boy would he. Right before he tackled her to the ground and handed her over to the guards.

"One less thing," Pern said cheerfully.

Rhys hastily finished his tea, said his goodbyes, and hurried out the door. Dark thoughts swarmed like bees in his brain. Zelaria had access to the ivy. She knew it was poisonous. She also had the skills to create the tincture and access to Lazys. The truth seemed so obvious but was also unexpected. The murderer and the mole had to be Zelaria. No wonder Lazys had committed suicide rather than answer; Zelaria was right there, standing beside them all. There was no question she was powerful enough to enchant the man to do her will.

Bile pooled in the back of his throat. It explained so much. Zelaria was the reason Eleanor even knew Tavyss was in Ouros. Why hadn't he thought of it before? She'd always wanted to be queen. His only question was why. If the Fates hadn't chosen her last time, why would she assume she'd be selected if Medea was killed?

He had to find Circe and send a falcon to intercept Medea and Tavyss if he could. They needed to know the truth. Whatever her motives, Zelaria was up to no good.

CHAPTER

THIRTEEN

On days like these, all Circe wanted to do was sleep. The sky outside Bloodgood's was an overcast gray. It was winter in the Dark Mountains, and the clouds threatened snow. But more than the weather was responsible for her foul mood. She'd had a bad feeling all day, a heaviness in the pit of her stomach that made her jolt every time the door opened. Overwhelmingly, she sensed that something bad was going to happen—or had happened, and soon she'd find out about it.

She couldn't wait for Rhys to get back from Franwise Farm so that she could do her part helping her sister. She planned to disguise herself in a dark cloak and shop the produce carts. It should be easy enough to put herself in a position to overhear conversations. The market was a den of gossip and innuendo. If people were discussing her sister, she'd hear. She might even learn who had poisoned her.

Business at Bloodgood's was as slow as usual. She sold a tonic for Beverly Coon's feverhound and healed a rash on Edi Smythe's arm, but two other customers walked out when they learned Rhys wasn't in, and one didn't even come in when he saw her behind the counter.

She hated that she was the cause of Rhys's business problems. Perhaps when things were settled with Tavyss and Paragon, and Medea was no longer queen, the people of Darnuith would accept her again as they did in their first days in the kingdom. Not that they were exceptionally kind or welcoming, but there was no hate before. She'd be happy with a return to indifference.

The bell above the door chimed, and Circe looked up to find Zelaria standing in the door, flanked by two royal soldiers. She was wearing purple robes in a style far too formal for the time of day, and her staff glowed with latent magic.

"Zelaria, what brings you here today?" The weight in her stomach grew heavier. "Did something happen to my sister?"

The witch's eyes turned hard and icy as a reptile's. "Seize her." The soldiers rushed forward.

Flustered, Circe didn't even think to draw her wand, just stared dumbfounded, not understanding what was happening. The guards bound her wrists. The only word she could manage was, "Why?"

"Circe Tanglewood, you are under arrest for aiding and abetting Queen Medea's act of treason."

"Treason?" Circe had no idea what the woman was talking about.

Zelaria pivoted and held the door open. "Bring her."

She was hauled roughly by the arms. "I don't understand. What's going on?"

Outside, she was thrust toward the open door of one of the royal carriages. She stuck out her foot and braced it on the door, making it impossible for the soldiers to force her inside. When Zelaria didn't answer her, Circe finally lost her temper. "I demand an explanation! When my sister hears about this—"

Zelaria gave a wicked laugh. "Oh, dear Circe, Medea and Tavyss are gone. Fled to Paragon, where Tavyss conspires to become king and then annex Darnuith using Medea's claim to the throne. The wizard council of Darnuith had already been notified. They will not succeed."

"That's not what's happening at all, and you know it!" Circe barked.

Zelaria drew her wand and sent a ball of orange light hurtling toward her head. Circe grunted as the magic plowed into her. Then everything went black.

CIRCE WOKE SOMEWHERE hard and cold, in a place with dank air that smelled of molding hay and animal dung. The lashes of her right eye brushed stone as she blinked, her face pressed into the floor. Slowly, she lifted her head, and the room came into focus.

"If you can stay asleep, I highly recommend it," Isis said somewhere behind her. "The real world isn't a fun place at the moment."

Circe pushed the rest of the way up. Isis was beside her, sitting on the stone floor with her knees pulled into her chest. "She got you too?"

"Yep."

"What is happening? Do you think Medea and Tavyss know what Zelaria is doing?"

"Shh." Isis's dark eyes flicked to the side. Circe followed her glance to a guard at the end of the hall. Isis threaded her fingers into her sister's.

Can you hear me?

Circe's eyes widened at the sound of her sister's voice inside her head. When had she learned to do that?

Something I read about in a book, she answered. *I've been practicing on Brody. We're in real danger here, sis. I think Zelaria is the one who told Eleanor about Tavyss and started this whole mess. If she's working with Paragon, this is a huge setup.*

"Why?" she asked.

Isis's gaze swiveled to the guard. "Concentrate on the connection," Isis whispered.

Circe narrowed her eyes and focused on the feel of Isis's hand in hers. The bond she shared with her sister was like no other. She sensed it now inside her like a string that traveled from within her to somewhere within her sister. She concentrated and silently pushed the words along it.

Why... would... she... do... that?

Good job. I can hear you. Isis nodded her approval. *With Medea out of the way, she probably thinks the Fates would choose her as the next queen.*

Circe shook her head and pushed the words through, faster this time. *Medea has the golden grimoire. She and Tavyss will grind Zelaria into dust the moment they return from Paragon.*

Isis squeezed her hand harder. *Don't you feel it? Try to sense Medea.*

She centered herself, reached out with her Tanglewood senses. They'd been born together, triplets with a magical bond forged in the womb. When she closed her eyes, she immediately sensed Isis like a black flame beside her, but Medea's light was harder to detect. Her light was weak, distant, flickering.

She's in trouble! We have to help her!

Yes, I feel that too. Medea and Tavyss traveled to Paragon on a peacekeeping mission to do exactly what Eleanor asked them to do. But they took everything the queen of Paragon said at face value. What if she was lying? What if they walked into a trap?

Circe bounded to her feet and paced the cell, wanting to blow out the walls. On an impulse, she grabbed the bars but screamed when a shock ran up both arms. The guard in the hall laughed at her. "Enchanted, sweetheart. Don't even try it."

She ignored him and slipped her hand back into Isis's. *How do we get out of here?*

They took our wands. Our cell is enchanted to keep us from using our magic. We need a plan. One that keeps our heads attached to our shoulders.

Circe glanced at the guard in the hall who'd laughed at her earlier. She suspected he could sense the power coming off them, even if he didn't quite know what they were doing. Most witches and wizards enjoyed a robust intuition about the use of magic. They were born with it.

"What's your name?" Circe asked him.

The man said nothing, just stared at her blankly.

"You know this is wrong. Medea has always treated you well. You have to let us out. Help us stop Zelaria."

The man pointed at his ears and shook his head. "Might as well stop flappin' your gums, witch. I can't hear a word of it. The enchantment on the bars mutes you. You can hear me, but I can't hear a word you say. Keeps inmates from casting incantations on their guards." He leaned back in his chair.

"Fuck!" Circe whirled, and this time when she addressed Isis, she didn't bother to do it in her head. "Any ideas, sister?"

Isis's already dark eyes turned black. "Brody won't notice I'm missing until tomorrow's hunt."

Circe folded her arms. "Rhys will notice I'm gone as soon as he gets back to Bloodgood's. There's no one tending the apothecary. He knows I would never just take off like this."

"He won't know to look for you here." Isis frowned.

"No." Circe drummed her fingers against her bicep.

Isis hung her head between her knees. "Yeah, I'd say we're totally screwed."

FOURTEEN

"Fates, what happened here?" Rhys landed his broom outside Bloodgood's, noticing deep, paw-shaped divots where a team of vultar hounds had stood in the street outside his apothecary. A scuffle of foot-prints led from a rumpled welcome mat to the place where ski marks grooved the snow. He had a bad feeling about this.

Rushing inside, he found the shop empty. "Circe?" He called up the stairs to her, but he knew in his gut she wasn't there. He was too late. If his theory was correct, Zelaria had likely come for her as soon as Medea had left the kingdom. Cursing, he ran into the storage room and started packing his basket. He had an idea of how to get her back, but it was going to take more than a bit of luck to see it through.

Once he had what he needed, he rushed back outside and mounted his broom, heading straight for Maelhaven Palace. If he was right about what was going on here, he'd find Circe and her sister in the dungeon. If he succeeded in freeing them—and that was a big if—they'd all have to act quickly to save Medea and Tavyss.

Even now as he soared over the Dark Mountains, he saw troops lining up at the Paragon border. He didn't fully understand why Zelaria would make that move, but he didn't like it. It almost looked like Darnuith was going to war.

He landed outside the front gate and smiled at the soldier at the guardhouse. He was relieved to see it was Neville Kent. He'd treated the boy before in his apothecary when he broke an arm as a child. Grown up now, he still had the same guileless expression he wore as a lad.

"Hello, Neville." Rhys gave an animated wave. "How's the elbow?"

The boy grinned back and swung his forearm around. "Good as new, thanks to you, Doc. What brings you by today?"

"Just delivering a few tonics for the palace stores." He gave Neville a bright smile.

"It's a bad time, Rhys. No one's up there but royal guards. Some weird stuff going on today. The queen's gone, and a bunch of my buddies were called to the border. Makes me nervous, like we're goin' ta war or somethin'. And there've been carriages coming and going, all secret-like."

Rhys shrugged. "Eh, you know me. I don't follow politics. Bad for the soul."

They laughed together.

"How is it that the troops can be called up anyway, if the queen isn't here? I thought she was the only one with that power."

Neville nodded like he'd thought the same. "I'm not supposed to talk about it…"

Rhys waited, tapping his basket.

"Keep it to yourself, but it turns out that if a queen is incapacitated or killed during her reign, her adviser takes on the role. My captain explained it to me. I guess the wizard's council is considering Medea incapacitated since she left with Tavyss for Paragon without clearing it with them. It's already been announced in the papers there. He's the rightful king, and he's taking back the throne."

"I hadn't heard," Rhys lied, keeping his voice flat.

Neville's head bobbed. "It's true. And the council is concerned. They say it's a conflict of interest, so they gave Zelaria Medea's powers. The queen has to be alive and present for the ritual of the Sacred Lots to work, you see. And it makes sense if you think about it. If someone assassinates the queen, her adviser will continue her rule as she planned it. Keeps other kingdoms from targeting her, hoping for change. And since, according to the council, Medea has effectively abandoned the kingdom by supporting Tavyss's rise to power, that puts Zelaria in charge."

The realization seized Rhys in an icy grip. Never in Rhys's life had a queen abdicated her position. No queen of Darnuith had ever been assassinated while on the throne. He'd forgotten the ins and outs of the laws concerning the position, the ones he'd learned in school and then never thought of again. Neville was right. One queen must name the next. Ferula had done it when she'd named Medea after the Fates had chosen her. If

Medea stepped down from her position as queen, the ritual of the Sacred Lots would happen again, and Medea would speak the name of her successor.

But if Medea was dead, she could not name her successor. That was why Zelaria had tried to kill her and pin it on Lazys. And when that plan hadn't worked, why she'd likely conspired with Eleanor to force Medea into a situation that would seem treasonous before the council. Fates, the council wouldn't even know Medea was in Paragon if not for Zelaria. She was behind it all.

Rhys kept a smile affixed to his face. "I'm sure it will all shake out in the end," he said cheerfully. He patted the basket on his hip. "Right, so, I was wondering if I might just bring this up to the castle and leave it for Zelaria, then? I hate to fly it all back to Bloodgood's if there's another option."

Neville thought about it for a moment. "Technically, I'm not supposed to let any guests through today, but I suppose you're not actually a guest but an employee of the palace at the moment. I'm sure it would be okay."

He inclined his head toward the boy. "Thank you. I'll owe you one."

Fates, he hoped he hadn't just made things difficult for the boy. As he strode quickly toward the mountaintop palace, he drew his wand and kept it close to his side. There was a guard at the door, unfortunately not someone he knew. That trick at the gate might not work with a stranger. Or, more likely, that soldier would follow him inside and ruin any hope he might have of finding Circe.

Thinking fast, he discreetly veered left, jaunting

around the side of the palace. There had to be a servant's entrance.

An elderly man in an apron stood outside a door, a pipe cradled in his palm. Rhys greeted him with a smile and wave. The man frowned and raised his smoke. "You shouldn't be—"

The petrification spell Rhys hit the man with came from the fastest draw of his wand and flick of his wrist he'd ever executed. He slipped past the old wizard, lying catatonic in the snow. "Sorry. Emergency."

Once inside the door, he padded straight for the dungeon, ducking behind pillars or into open doors every time he saw another face. Fates, what he would do for an invisibility spell right about now. Hidden, in an alcove off the back hall, he spied a guard outside the door to the dungeon. Magic might set off wards inside the palace, but he had other ways to get past the man. He dug in his bag.

A moment later, he strode forward, beaming and waving. "There you are!" he said in his friendliest tone.

The guard, another he did not know, rose from his chair and placed a hand on his sword. "Who are you? What are you doing back here?"

"Zelaria sent me. I'm a healer. Turns out you need a bit of this." He slapped an herb-soaked cloth over the man's nose and mouth. The man thrashed and kicked while Rhys clung to him like he was a green colt. He let out an oomph as an elbow landed in his gut and almost let go when the guard stomped on his toes. Bigger and stronger he might be, but the herbs worked quickly, thank the Fates. The guard finally slumped to the floor.

Limping, Rhys pulled the keys from the guard's belt and entered the dungeon, dragging the body inside with him before locking the door again. When he turned around, a wand was pointed at his head.

"Don't move," the guard hissed. His gaze darted to the other guard, heaped on the floor at his feet.

"I'm a healer," Rhys said. "He passed out, and I was about to administer a tonic."

The man wasn't buying it. "Why would you drag him in here to administer a tonic?"

Rhys couldn't answer that question. He studied the man, then finally looked beyond his wand. Circe and Isis were there, in the cell! He looked back at the guard. "Don't I know your mother? I think she comes into Bloodgood's from time to time. You're the Rintwood boy." He worked his hand into the side pouch of his basket.

"No. Family's Blackett—"

Rhys flung the open vial toward the guard's mouth, then ducked. A red blast erupted above his head as the man doubled over, spitting. "What the Fates was—" The man didn't finish his sentence. He froze, then toppled over on his side.

"Neurotoxin. Sorry, Mr. Blackett. You'll be fine in an hour."

He rushed to the cell where Circe and Isis were jumping up and down and yelling something he couldn't hear. He rummaged through the keys, trying each one until the door finally gave.

"Fates, I love you," Circe cried when she finally made

it through the open door. She pulled him against her and kissed him like he was the god of love himself.

"Worth every broken toe." He slanted a grin in her direction.

"Broken toe?"

"No time. We've got to get out of here before our friends wake up."

Isis was already across the dungeon, digging in the guard's pockets. "We need our wands."

Rhys frowned. "Fuck. Are they even down here?"

"They took mine from me right before they locked me up." She felt along the man's chest and then moved to the other guard who'd been by the door.

"What about yours?" he asked Circe.

"I was unconscious. Don't even remember."

"He knocked you out? I'll kill him."

"Not him. Zelaria. Hit me with a sleeping charm."

He ground his teeth.

"Found them!" Isis tossed Circe's wand to her, her dark eyes blazing.

"Quickly," Rhys said. "We'll have to run for it."

Circe took his hand. "No need. Isis?"

"Got it." She grabbed his other hand and circled her wand above her head. True fear gripped Rhys as the shadows in the dungeon melted from the walls and rushed at him like a dark wind. Darkness swallowed him, knocked the breath from his lungs. All he could think was that he'd become the night itself and was being channeled through a cramped and lightless space.

The next second, he was standing in the snow in the

shadow of a mountain a half mile outside Maelhaven Palace grounds.

"That was a neat trick," he said, coughing.

"Comes in handy when you're being charged by elderbeasts," Isis said.

Circe shivered in the mountain chill. "My sister can command shadows, as well as other things." Her teeth clacked together in the cold. Rhys realized that neither of them had coats. Not surprising, considering how Zelaria had rounded them up.

"Where to now?" Isis asked. "I think Medea is in real trouble."

"There's something I need to tell you." Rhys pulled Circe against him and wrapped the sides of his coat around her. He regretted he couldn't do the same for Isis, but before they moved on, both of them needed to know what he'd learned. As fast as he could, he relayed what Pern Franwise had said about Zelaria. "I think Medea and Tavyss were set up. I think Zelaria was responsible for poisoning Medea, and she's used Tavyss's claim to the throne of Paragon as a reason to challenge her position."

"But Medea planned to step down anyway," Circe said. "Why would Zelaria do that?"

Isis's dark stare pierced right through him, and he could tell the moment she understood. She was not as softhearted as Circe.

"Because she wants to be queen," Isis said darkly.

Rhys nodded. "If Medea is painted as a traitor or dies, Zelaria becomes queen. The ritual of the Sacred Lots cannot be performed if Medea is dead or has abandoned her throne."

Isis seethed. "I knew there was something up with that witch."

"She already has troops lined up at the border. Most of them don't even know why they are there. It's all a setup. I suspect she'd been working with Eleanor this entire time. If there's a scuffle... Zelaria will benefit if Medea is killed."

"Zelaria's always wanted to be queen," Circe said, shaking her head. "Why didn't we think of this before? It was no secret how much it stung when the Fates named Medea."

Isis scoffed. "We didn't think of it because Medea trusted her. Zelaria helped her a lot in the early days. How was she to know the witch was just biding her time?"

Circe fisted her hands and yelled in frustration toward the heavens. "She poisoned Medea," Circe said incredulously. "I always knew Zelaria was strange and off-putting, but she'd never struck me as a murderer."

Isis frowned at her sister. "She never struck us as someone who would throw us in the dungeon either. She had us arrested for aiding Medea's treason. *Treason*, Circe. If Rhys hadn't rescued us, we'd have been executed."

Rhys stared at the profile of the woman he loved as her disbelief melted away, replaced by horrified acceptance. She leaned into his chest. He tried to sound confident as he said, "For Zelaria's plan to work, Medea and

Tavyss have to play into her and Eleanor's plans. We have to prevent them from taking the bait. The only way to stop her is to go to Paragon and keep Tavyss from announcing his intention to be king. If we do that, there is no catalyst for violence. If we can get them out alive and return Medea to Darnuith, she can deny Zelaria's claims. We can make the council listen and set things right."

FIFTEEN

"Medea told me the announcement was to be made after the banquet tonight. They're already in the palace. How will we get to them in time? The Obsidian Guard isn't going to let us through the front gate uninvited." Circe looked between Isis and Rhys, desperate to save her sister.

Rhys scratched the stubble on his jaw. "At one time, you mentioned that you were an expert in transformation like your namesake."

"I am," Circe said.

Isis agreed. "She's the best I've ever seen."

Rhys raised an eyebrow. "The wards around the Obsidian Palace aren't designed to keep out animals."

Eyes widening, Circe turned to Isis. "Can you get us to Hobble Glen?"

She gave a certain nod. "It will take a few hops to cover the distance, and it will be draining, but I can do it."

"Then get us there. I'll do the rest." They joined

hands, and the shadow of the mountain reached out, swirled around them, and carried them away.

An hour later, Circe found herself in the woods outside Hobble Glen, near the guard tower of the Obsidian Palace. Thankfully, it was warm here, but with Paragon's sacred mountain looming over them, the temperature was the least of her worries. She gathered her strength and told the others her plan. "As smart as Rhys's plan was, it doesn't make sense for me to transform all three of us. If I transform myself into an animal, I won't be able to hold my wand properly to transform myself back, and by the time my transfiguration wears off on its own, it may be too late."

Rhys narrowed his eyes. "Then how do you plan to get us all inside?"

"Last time we were here, I noticed their carriages were pulled by Paragonian mountainhorses instead of vultar hounds. They don't use dogs. I'm going to transform you into the most shining example of Darnuithian canines they've ever seen and present you at the door as gifts from the king and queen of Paragon."

Rhys exchanged glances with Isis as if he wasn't at all sure about this situation, but he gave her a nod of acceptance.

"Undress and put your clothes and wands in Rhys's basket. I'll carry it in." Circe raised her wand and started centering herself, finding the right incantation in her head. She pictured the royal hounds that had pulled their carriage their first time here. When she opened her eyes again, she smiled at the way her sister and Rhys stood awkwardly among the trees, looking anywhere but at each other. She put them out of their misery.

"*Metamorfóno!*" She circled the tip of her wand in the air and snapped her wrist toward Rhys. His body sprouted a coat of shaggy black hair, and his nose and mouth stretched into a snout filled with razor-sharp teeth. He blinked red eyes at her.

"Handsome even as a dog," she whispered, scratching his ear.

"Give me a break." Isis rolled her eyes.

Circe flashed an impish grin before casting the same spell in her sister's direction. Isis transformed into a vultar hound with a shaggy white coat. Together, the two were a striking match. She slipped the basket over her shoulder and then transfigured Rhys's belt and Isis's necklace into two jewel-studded collars and leashes. After fastening them easily around the necks of Rhys and Isis—who looked as if she might bite her—Circe led the two out of the woods and up the main road toward the palace grounds.

"Greetings," she said cheerfully to the man in the tiny house. "I am Ruth Vestar here to deliver a gift to the king and queen of Paragon from the witch queen of Darnuith."

The man frowned. "I don't have you on the list."

"Of course you don't. What kind of surprise would it be if your king and queen knew it was coming? This is the way of our people." Circe lifted her chin.

The soldier, dressed in red and black, cracked his neck and stared down at the dogs with a look of annoyance. "I'll have to send a falcon to the palace to get permission."

"Please do," Circe said, but inside, she was worried. They couldn't afford to waste any more time. As soon as the man looked away to whistle for a falcon, she pretended to fall and pushed both dogs forward, releasing their leashes. "Oh! Oh dear! I lost my grip."

The guardsman groaned as the dogs ran full speed toward the palace. Circe gave him a desperate look and did her best to cast her influence over the dragon. "They will come to me. Please, allow me to pass and collect them."

The male studied her. By the look on his face, he found her lacking in every way, which was a good thing because he immediately and thoroughly underestimated her.

"Go ahead through," he grumbled. "I don't have time for this," he added under his breath.

Circe made a show of thanking him as she crossed the wards and wandered inside, her vapid expression morphing into one of determination as she chased the dogs around the side of the palace. She caught up to them and picked up their leashes.

"Good work. Now, to get inside," she mumbled.

As it turned out, that feat wasn't a problem at all because at that moment, an explosion rocked the palace.

Chaos broke loose around her. Red and black uniforms ran past her as fiery blasts blew from the mountain above. The ground rumbled. Rhys and Isis tugged her by the wrists into the gardens, where she hid among the foliage. She quickly slipped the collars from their necks. "*Metamorfóno!*"

Opening the basket, she tossed their clothing and wands at them. Heart thumping in her chest, she stared, dumbfounded, as people ran in all directions. Rhys, back to his normal form, grabbed her wrist and pointed toward the door. Unattended. If there had been a guard, he'd fled from whatever was causing the explosions. Screams peppered the twilight.

"What's going on?" Circe's heart clenched for Medea. Isis appeared beside her, fully dressed. Shadows clung to her like a second skin.

"I sense death inside," she said darkly.

Circe jogged through the door and up the way they'd come before, hugging the shadows. A guard ran past them but didn't stop. He didn't seem to see them in his haste to exit the building.

"Do you feel that?" Rhys asked.

"Dread," Isis said. "A witch has spelled these dragons to feel fear."

They reached the Great Mountain Hall just as another dragon burst from its doors, fleeing in a panic. Rhys slipped his foot inside the closing door. Circe peeked through the crack and gasped at the horror inside. Blood sprayed the walls. Everywhere, bodies lay strewn across the ballroom.

"This would go faster if you helped," Brynhoff barked, sword in hand.

Eleanor came into view and kicked one of the bodies in the side. "Don't be a fool. I have to keep watch to make sure none of them recovers. If someone rouses, I can administer another dose of the witch's poison."

Brynhoff hesitated. "I still don't understand how we'll pin this on them if they're dead."

"Every person who left this room has a memory planted in their head of Tavyss and Medea orchestrating this massacre and you heroically ending them. Zelaria planted it herself. Now, get back to work. The faster you kill them, the faster we can put this terrible mess behind us."

Circe's breath was stolen from her lungs as Brynhoff's sword sliced through the air toward the neck of one of the fallen. Blood sprayed. The body turned to ash, and a jewel the size of a man's fist clanked across the floor.

Blinded by rage, she raised her wand, ready to unleash her magical fury on them, but Rhys's hand clamped over her mouth. He dragged her backward into an alcove in the veranda. The shiny black floor reflected her struggle against his grip. "Stop, Circe. They'll kill you too. The three of us are no match for two dragons. They'll swallow us in dragon fire. We need a distraction."

She looked to Isis, but her sister's face was vacant, painfully still. Within a white-knuckled grip, she held her wand, the tip glowing red as Hades. Circe's teeth ground together as she met Rhys's gaze. "Hurry," was all she said.

Rhys dug in his basket and pulled out two vials half full of clear liquid. He popped off the tops with his thumbs. "Wait here." He poured one into the other and then threw it around the corner, down the hall that led past the Great Mountain Hall and into the palace proper.

The glass tinkled as it cracked against the obsidian. Rhys sprinted back to Circe and corralled her and Isis against the wall. The boom that followed shook the slab of rock under their feet.

Brynhoff and Eleanor's panicked voices came a moment later.

"Was that one of ours?" Eleanor asked.

"No. All of the charges we planned detonated earlier," Brynhoff hissed.

"Check the hall," the queen ordered. "I'll check the throne room. We can't have any loose ends, Brynhoff. Darnuith's troops will wage an attack at any moment. This has to look like Darnuith initiated it."

"I'm not an idiot, Eleanor," he snapped.

"Just go." Circe heard footsteps and then the sound of the hallway entrance opening and closing.

Rhys removed his arms from her and crept back to the door, peeking inside. He waved them in. Circe could not believe her eyes. Dragons lay in bloody heaps, splayed across the floor. Large gemstones littered the space between the bodies. Blood sprayed the rows of chairs. This wasn't just a murder. It was a massacre.

"Are those *hearts*?" Isis asked, staring at the gems.

"I think so," Rhys said. He placed fingers on the neck of one of the dragons. "Eleanor has poisoned them, but poison isn't enough to kill a dragon. These others will recover if they aren't beheaded before they wake up."

"That's what Brynhoff was doing. I heard them say so before." Circe gasped, realizing something more. "This is the meeting of the Council of Elders Medea referred to. Oh my god, Eleanor and Brynhoff poisoned all of them and are staging this to blame the murders on Medea and Tavyss!"

"Fates," her sister cursed. "I found Medea!"

Circe ran to Isis's side, and all the air rushed from her lungs. Medea lay motionless on the obsidian floor, eyes open and staring at the ceiling. Every happy feeling Circe had ever felt seemed to drain from her body. Her sister was dead.

Rhys reached into his apothecary bag and retrieved the poison antidote he'd used before, but when he tried to tip it into her mouth, he pulled back his hand at the feel of her skin. "It's too late. She's... cold."

Circe dropped to her knees, a sob catching in her throat. "How is this possible? I thought... She told us Tavyss's tooth made her immortal!"

But Isis had already figured it out. She squatted between the bodies and picked up a yellow jewel larger than her fist.

"Is that...a dragon's heart?" Circe swallowed the lump that formed in her throat.

Isis gave her a knowing nod. "Tavyss is dead. They killed him first." The shadows in the room gathered around her, hugging her sides like old friends. She slipped the heart into Rhys's basket.

Circe released a trembling breath. Right, they couldn't leave the heart...here. She stared down at Medea. She didn't want to leave her here either. This was her sister. Dead or alive, she should remain with a Tanglewood. Her body must come with them.

"Bring Medea," Isis said to Rhys. "We need to get her somewhere safe."

Thank the Fates Isis had the same idea. Circe hooked her fingers under Medea's arms and started dragging her toward the exit, her shoes slipping in puddles of dragon blood. "Rhys, help me.

"They'll notice she's gone." Rhys's voice cracked. "There's nothing you can do. She's already dead."

Isis pinned him with a dark and dangerous stare. "Don't tell me what I can and cannot do, Rhys Bloodgood." She strode toward the exit, the shadows trailing behind her. The darkness seemed to whisper to her sister in a way that sent a chill through Circe. Isis checked the hall then looked back at them over her shoulder. "The way is clear. Bring Medea. Quickly. I have a plan."

CHAPTER

SIXTEEN

Rhys scooped Medea into his arms at Circe's urging. A sense of doom lingered in his gut, and the hair on his arms stood on end. He hadn't been this close to death since he'd lost June. Did Circe feel the same way he'd felt then? Disbelief. Anger. The temptation to undo what had been done. Dark thoughts such as those had stolen his breath in the early days.

Oddly, he did not see grief on Isis's or Circe's faces. Instead, he saw vicious resolve. Whatever Isis was planning, it sounded dark and probably dangerous. The moment she'd seen Medea's body, she'd visibly changed. Death seemed to cling to her. She wore it like a royal mantle.

Unnerving as it was, he followed Isis out the way they'd come, Circe at his side. The halls were empty aside from the echoes of Eleanor and Brynhoff bickering about the charge Rhys had set off in the hall on the other side of the ballroom. As fast as he could move with Medea's dead weight in his arms, he rushed after Isis and Circe, anxious to put distance between them and the palace. If the king and queen discovered Medea was missing...

"There, the forest." Isis pointed into a dense wood to the southwest, in the direction of the Sanguine River. Rhys followed after her until they were deep within a thicket of trees.

"Isis, I think we're beyond the palace wards," Circe said. "I can't feel them any longer."

Rhys halted. "The wards are built to keep trespassers out, not in." He rested Medea's body on a bed of moss. "We're not safe, though. When Eleanor notices her body is gone—"

"Medea will be back from the dead and able to take her revenge," Isis said darkly. The shadows tangled around her like vipers.

"Back from the dead?" Rhys looked to Circe, his head spinning. "What are you saying?"

But Circe did not assuage his fears. Her face was grim as she asked, "Can you do it, sister?"

"I can," Isis said. "I've done it before."

"With birds and sheep. Never people." Circe placed a hand on her heart. "Are you sure?"

Isis scoffed. "You were born with a talent for transfiguration. Medea for enchantments. I was born with power over life and death. I am certain, sister. I feel her clinging to the space in between here and the next world. I must pull her back now, or she'll move on."

"Do it," Circe said.

A chill prickled Rhys's skin. Oh, how he remembered wanting to resurrect June! He'd considered it in his grief. What few magical texts he could find on the subject all warned against it. Every wizard he'd approached denied him help. He'd heard horrific stories. "It's unnatural. It's forbidden to raise the dead."

Isis ignored him. She felt along the neck of Medea's gown until she fisted the queen's diamond pendant and pulled it over her head. According to Circe, that gem held the golden grimoire—Hera's grimoire—the one Circe claimed could flatten Paragon to dust.

Rhys tried again, raising his hands. "Listen to me. I know you want her back. I know. When my wife died, I found the spells. I thought about trying it. But there's a reason it's forbidden. There is always a price to such magic. Always."

Isis's pupils were abnormally large and black as night. "Then let Eleanor pay it."

Circe drew her wand. "Stand back, Rhys. We're doing this."

Magic thickened the air around him, and Rhys backed away. What they were doing was wrong, but no potion or tonic in his basket could change the sisters' minds, and the power they were putting off was well beyond his abilities. He might be able to stop Circe, simply by overpowering her physically, but those shadows Isis was stirring held a menace he didn't even understand. Rhys was a man who knew how to pick his battles, and this was not one he could win.

Isis held the stone up to the light and turned it, gazing into its depths. Clouds rolled in overhead, and mist formed around their ankles. The air smelled earthy and dank, like the inside of a cave.

"I have it." Isis handed the stone to Circe, who held it

up toward the moon. When she lowered it again, she gave him a hard look.

"Don't interfere, Rhys."

He shook his head. He loved her. It was done. There was no choice, really. He didn't agree with what she was doing, but he wouldn't undermine her.

She picked up a stick and used it to carve a symbol in the earth around her sister, drawing intricate patterns inside it.

"We need her wand," Isis said.

Circe dug in Medea's sleeve. "It's still here. Fates, she never even had a chance to draw it."

Trumpets sounded behind him. Rhys whirled. He pulled his enchanted glasses from his basket and looked toward the Dark Mountains. Black-robed witches floated on their brooms in formation along the border to Paragon, the tips of their wands glowing like stars.

Darnuith's army had taken flight.

"Darnuith is attacking Paragon," he said. "We need to go."

Isis barely glanced in his direction.

"I know you're grieving, but things could get far more difficult for us very soon," Rhys said. A war between dragons and witches would be deadly, whether it was staged by Zelaria and Eleanor or not.

Without even glance in his direction, Circe laid Medea's wand along her breastbone. The sisters started to circle. The shadows around their ankles stretched and tangled with their movements, growing thick. Isis whispered an incantation in a strange language Rhys had never heard before. Medea's body began to glow. With perfect orchestration, Circe dropped Tavyss's heart toward Medea's chest, and Isis drew her wand across her wrist like her veins were the strings of a macabre violin. Blood shed into that glowing light. It splashed over the dragon heart, over their sister's chest.

The power the spell created gusted his hair back in a gale force wind. It grew in intensity until his feet slid across the forest floor and he had to cling to a tree to hold himself in place. Lightning sliced through the previously calm night sky, and a crack of thunder rattled his bones. The second boom made his ears ring and threw him to the ground. It sounded as if their entire world had cracked in two.

He screamed and clung to the forest floor, unable to move against the torrential flood of power raging over him. When the storm of fire finally settled, he raised his head, surprised the trees around them were still standing. Circe lay a few feet away, limbs splayed. He crawled to her through thick mist. She was breathing, thank the Fates.

"Isis," she said.

The mist parted just enough for them to see her leaning over Medea, cradling the dead woman's head in her outstretched arms. Shadows twisted and coiled around her in the darkness, tangling with the mist so that even by the full moon he could barely see Medea's body. Serpents of darkness. Thousands of them covered Medea's body, writhing and tangling with one another until he could no longer see Medea at all.

Isis's eyes glowed red as hot embers.

His breath caught. Something had moved under

those long, black things. The shadows and mist expanded and contracted over Medea. The night was breathing. The darkness had a heartbeat. Pressure throbbed against his skin, popped his ears.

Circe gripped his arms and leaned into him, shivering. He didn't deny her the comfort of his embrace.

"Tavyss?" Medea's strangled voice came from under the mist. She cried out the dragon's name with such pain, Rhys pulled Circe closer. But she gently extracted herself from his grip and walked to her sisters on trembling legs.

Rhys couldn't stand. His knees were shaking too hard. In all his years as a wizard, he'd never witnessed a resurrection. A whiff of sulfur met his nose, and his heart pounded as if he were standing at the gates to Hades itself.

All at once, the shadows drained away like water after a rain, and there she was. Medea stared at him with vibrant blue eyes and pink cheeks. He released a trembling breath. These were no ordinary witches. These three sisters held the magic of the old gods in their blood. No wonder the Fates had chosen Medea. She'd held the formula for life itself around her neck.

"Medea!" Circe knelt beside her and threw her arms around her neck, pulling her close. "Thank the Fates. It worked! Oh, Isis, it worked."

Isis smiled, and all the shadows dissipated. Her eyes morphed from blood red to deep blue. She hugged her sister from the opposite side.

"Tavyss?" Medea asked, her voice strained.

Isis searched the ground around her body and

retrieved the golden jewel that was his heart. She held it out to her sister. "I'm so sorry, Medea, but his soul has moved on to wherever it is dragon souls go," Isis said. "I cannot resurrect him. He is no longer... here." She motioned to his heart. "And he was not in any dimension of the underworld."

Medea convulsed into sobs, the heart clutched to her chest. Rhys thought he'd be torn apart by the grief that rolled off her in waves and triggered his own dark memories. But after several minutes, she quieted and her tear-etched face took on an angry edge. Her voice was cold and hard as steel as she said, "It was a trap. Eleanor and Brynhoff invited us all onto the veranda for a toast. We were all given glasses of Tribiscal wine. Tavyss made his announcement, and everyone drank. I thought the wine was safe because we chose our own glass from among dozens. We were surrounded by well-wishers." The words came out like a punch. "But Eleanor and Brynhoff poisoned their entire Council of Elders and us along with them. *Why*? I can't figure out why they would do that."

Rhys looked back at where he'd seen Darnuith's troops on the horizon. The witches were gone, but dragons patrolled the skies above Hobble Glen. "Why? Because you were set up by Zelaria. You can't return to Darnuith, my queen."

Medea's weeping red eyes sought him out.

He licked his lips before continuing his explanation. "Zelaria and Eleanor orchestrated this. The slaying of the Council of Elders will be blamed on you and Tavyss."

"Everyone knows we were there at Eleanor's invitation! People saw—"

"Who? The people who are dead? They're all dead, my queen. And the servants, the guards... When we left with you, they were in a stupor. Zelaria has enchanted them to believe you were behind this." He pointed toward the witches, rising like a cloud above the dark mountains. "She and Eleanor are staging a war... a war that will be blamed on you and will result in your death and the deaths of the entire Council of Elders."

"Dear Fates." Circe clutched at her throat. "We have to stop Zelaria. She needs to pay for this."

"My well is dry, sister," Isis said. Indeed, the witch appeared waifish and depleted in every way.

Medea opened her mouth to say something to her, then stopped abruptly and looked down at herself. Her face turned white as bone. As she climbed to her feet, her hand trembled along her perfectly flat abdomen.

Rhys's eyes stung, and he shook his head at Isis. "I told you there would be a price."

"My-my son. My son!" Medea bent in half and vomited.

"I didn't know!" Isis cried. "The shadows brought you back. I thought he'd come with you."

The full horror of the situation tore at Rhys's heart. Medea was no longer pregnant. Her son had moved on when she'd died, and when the shadows had brought her back and knit her flesh under that writhing mass of darkness, it was without him. It was as if he had never been.

Could there be anything worse than losing a child

having never known him? To wake up to find him gone. Taken from her before she could ever hold him, look upon him. Rhys wondered how she could bear it. Maybe she couldn't. Medea collapsed onto her hands and knees, her grief pouring out of her in wretched sobs.

Somewhere in the distance, a dragon roared.

"We need to find a place to hide." Rhys's voice cracked. He couldn't allow himself to spiral with Medea, not until they were safe. "Somewhere we can rest and make a plan."

"Where can we go?" Circe asked, her expression pleading.

"Brody might take us in," Isis whispered. "Or we could shelter in the Ice Forest. The demon who lives there keeps visitors away."

Rhys shook his head. "I don't think we should risk Darnuith. I have a friend from Rogos—"

"Daluk, the scribe," Circe remembered. "You said you've been working with him on the gila vine problem."

"I have, and I have the antidote with me, along with the serum to control the vine's growth. I planned to deliver it to him after I visited with Pern and Viktor Franwise, but I never got the chance. He'll want what I have. He'll help us."

Circe turned to her sister. "Isis, are you strong enough to take us there by shadow?"

Isis shook her head. "I told you. I'm drained. I'm barely strong enough to carry myself twenty steps."

"I left my broom at the palace when I rescued you," Rhys said. "We can't fly."

Medea wiped under her swollen eyes. "We can take

the Sanguine River. It's neutral territory, and the cargo ships are notorious for taking bribes."

"My queen, everyone knows who you are. Even with a bribe, you're conspicuous. Eleanor will top anything we offer." Rhys frowned at Medea's gown. She was covered in blood from the ritual, and before, when the dragons around her were slain. All of them were smeared with it from handling her body.

"Circe..." Medea met her sister's eyes with an unasked question.

Circe nodded. "I can do it." She waved her wand, and Medea transformed. The gown she was wearing turned into a commoner's tunic and leggings. Her nose broadened, and her hair paled from deep black to a rich shade of honey.

Medea looked down at herself and cleared her throat. "Problem solved."

A dragon-shaped shadow passed between them and the moon. "We need to move. I think it smells us." Rhys helped Medea to her feet.

All at once, tree branches snapped, and a bark-colored dragon tore through the forest in front of them. Its purple heart glowed as its lungs filled with fire. Rhys braced himself to be burned to a crisp.

"*Cogitatio!*" Medea yelled, crossing her arms. Fire blasted toward them, then stopped, curving around Medea's magical shield. How was she doing this? She had to be weak given what she'd just been through, and she was projecting a shield large enough to protect them all.

Eventually, the dragon's fire petered out, and Medea dropped her shield, panting.

Circe flicked her wand, and a spell shot bright purple from the tip. The dragon transformed into a rat who coughed a harmless puff of smoke. Rhys gaped at her in unapologetic wonder.

"It won't last," she yelled. "Dragons are resistant to magic!"

Even as he watched, the rat's eyes glowed purple and its fur transformed into scales. He grabbed Circe's hand. "Run!"

CHAPTER
SEVENTEEN

As Circe had predicted, the spell didn't last. The only reason it worked at all was that she'd practiced on Tavyss and understood dragon anatomy enough to aim for the vulnerable space between the scales near his heart. Still, it wasn't enough. She could hear the dragon roaring behind them as they sprinted toward the river that separated Paragon from Nochtbend.

But it was dark in the woods. The moon wasn't enough to breach the thick cover of the forest, and she tripped over the uneven ground. Rhys helped her up and then tripped himself. They leaned on each other, hearts pounding and drenched with sweat, until the trees finally parted and the river came into view.

Next to a bridge that crossed from the kingdom of Paragon to the kingdom of Nochtbend was a small port used for trade, and just as Medea had hypothesized, a boat waited there. There was a man on the deck, staring in their direction as if he could see them clearly, although they moved silently and in shadow. It bothered her, this unnatural sight. Only when they drew nearer did Circe realize why it troubled her so much. The creature was neither dragon nor witch. This, she realized, was a citizen of Nochtbend. A vampire.

The man was stunning, as if the night had woven a body for itself out of dreams and stars. His hair was black, as were his eyes, his skin as pale as the moon above his head. Full red lips framed a proportionally wide mouth that balanced out the relative size of his eyes. All together with an exceedingly fit physique, he was a sight that drew her magnetically, in a way that could only be explained by magic.

Medea stormed forward, not an ounce of fear in her eyes. "We need passage to Rogos. I can pay you, handsomely."

The man leaped from the deck of his ship and was directly in front of her in the blink of an eye. Circe hadn't even heard a single footstep or the creak of a board on the dock. "And what will you pay me with, witch? Do you assume I desire money from you?" He leaned toward her and sniffed the skin of her neck. Medea didn't even flinch.

"How is she so strong?" Circe whispered to Rhys.

He said nothing but drew his wand and moved in behind Medea, backing her up. Circe and Isis did the same, although Isis could conjure barely a wisp of a shadow. The vampire didn't so much as glance in their direction but held Medea's stare with unmistakable curiosity.

"Your blood sings with magic but reeks of death and grief." He scowled as if the last two offended him. "What has befallen you this night... Queen Medea?"

"I don't know what you are talking about. My name is Freta."

"How?" Circe whispered to Rhys. Medea's disguise was foolproof. She doubted she'd recognize her own sister in it.

But the vampire was sure of himself. "Your name is Medea Tanglewood, and you are queen of Darnuith." His strange reflective eyes snapped to Circe. "Your transfiguration is good, witch, but after centuries, I do not trust my eyes. It's her scent that gives her away. I smell Maelhaven on you. Snow, elderbeast, vultar hound."

Medea scowled. "What do you want of me, vampire? We need passage."

"Never fear. You are the reason I came here tonight. Rumors rarely slip past vampire ears, you understand. Things whispered in the dead of night are heard by the darkness, and we are the darkness. I wondered if I'd ever meet you. You've been secretive since you took your throne."

"I had reason to be."

"Where is your consort?" he asked as if he knew.

"Dead. Murdered by Eleanor and Brynhoff."

"I suspected they wouldn't give up power so easily."

"We seek passage to Rogos. Please." She took his hands, and Circe cringed. At the touch of her fingers, the vampire's fangs dropped, and his eyes locked on to her sister's throbbing pulse.

Rhys raised his wand. "Don't get any ideas," he said.

Circe felt a breeze on her cheek, and the wand was gone. Rhys gaped at his empty hand. The vampire twirled it between his fingers. "Don't threaten me, wizard, especially considering I am your way to Rogos."

A roar came from behind them, and Circe looked over her shoulder. The dragon had recovered. It flew toward them in the distance. "Fates, we're out of time!"

"I will require a favor from you, Medea, in the future."

She didn't hesitate. "You have it!"

He moved aside and gestured for them to climb aboard. They sprinted onto the boat, and the vampire pushed it from the dock before leaping on board and firing up the engine. The dragon passed low over their heads.

"Why isn't it burning us to a crisp?" Isis asked.

"It can't. This is a royal vessel of Nochtbend in neutral waters. If he so much as scratches the hull, it could be considered an act of war. I don't know that soldier, but I suspect that sort of call is beyond his pay grade."

With a roar of frustration, the dragon banked, its leathery wings flapping as it soared back toward Paragon.

"Royal vessel?" Circe turned toward the vampire, who was still staring at Medea as if he was absolutely enchanted by her.

"Allow me to introduce myself. I am Master Demidicus, supreme leader of the Nochtbend coven." He took

Medea's hand, brushed back the tails of his black jacket, and bowed regally to plant a kiss on her wrist. "Now, if you would join me, I'd like to discuss something with you in private." He gestured toward the helm of the ship, where another vampire was steering the vessel. Medea indicated for the rest of them to stay back and followed Demidicus to the bow of the ship.

"I need to find a place to lie down," Isis said in a low, raspy voice. She looked spent, and Circe gave her shoulder a supportive squeeze as she lumbered toward the rear of the boat and the pallets of cargo there.

"What do you think he's saying to her?" Rhys asked, glancing at Medea and Demidicus, who were engaged in lively and amicable conversation behind the window of the helm.

"Probably telling her what he wants in payment." Circe frowned. "It must not be too terrible. Is she laughing?"

"Appears so." Rhys rubbed a hand along her back. "I don't get the sense that it's her blood. He could have taken that if he wanted it. Probably a political favor or a magical one. Vampires are phenomenally powerful but can't perform magic. Maybe he needs a spell."

All the intensity of the night hit her at once, and she sagged against him. "Oh, Rhys. Tavyss... the baby. It's too much. My heart can't bear it."

"Come." He led her between the pallets to one that looked clean and soft. They sank down to the deck and leaned against the white fabric bundles.

"I still can't believe what Zelaria did. I—"

"Shh. It's been a long, hard night, Circe. Rest. The dead will still be dead tomorrow, and the living will still be living. There will be time enough to sort it all out then."

She nodded sleepily, leaned into his chest, and closed her eyes.

EIGHTEEN

Silver light rimmed the horizon by the time the river opened into the sea. Rhys recognized Asfolk Palace gleaming in pink marble splendor off the coast of Rogos. The cargo ship they were on had no comfortable lodging, but he and Circe had slept off and on, propped against one of the pallets the vampire was carrying on deck. Rhys wasn't sure what was in the canvas bag he'd used as a pillow, but it put off an herbal scent when he moved his head that was thankfully not unpleasant.

He'd barely opened his eyes when Demidicus's long, bony fingers landed on his shoulder. "The sun is rising, wizard. We must dock here for the day." Demidicus's fangs were out, and his face was disturbingly close. The vampire's gaze lingered on his throat. Rhys was just happy he seemed to be ignoring Circe, who was still asleep on his chest.

"I've got it covered," Rhys said, swallowing hard. "I have a friend in Rogos. I can lead them to him."

"Good."

"Where will you be?"

The vampire's already wide mouth spread until it seemed to show an unnatural number of teeth. "A vampire never reveals where he sleeps, Rhys Bloodgood of Bloodgood's Apothecary, and he always remembers where you do."

"Understood." Rhys watched the vampire stroll back to the helm, where his accomplice guided the boat into port and cut the engine. The two vampires dissolved into the night as if they could disappear with it, melting into shadow as the light took hold. There was no trace of them by the time the first rays from the dual suns of Ouros broke the horizon.

"Circe, wake up. We're here." He shook her gently by the shoulder.

She rose sleepily, and together they went in search of the others. They found Isis in a deep, restorative sleep on what looked like a stack of bolts of fabric. Once they'd collected her, they found Medea asleep in the helm. She'd been given a sleeping bag and a pillow. Rhys almost hated to wake her. A smile tugged at the corner of her lips, and he worried that consciousness would bring with it memories of her loss and the grief that had crushed her the night before. But she woke on her own, seeming to sense them there.

"It's time to go, isn't it?" Her eyes fluttered open, and her smile faded, replaced by an expression formed of determination and hardened grief.

"I'm sorry," Rhys said. He didn't know what else to say.

"Don't be sorry for me," she said. "I understand now

how things are." She stood and turned her face to the rising suns. "Demidicus helped me to see it."

Isis snorted. "The vampire helped you... emotionally?"

She nodded. "Vampires are dead. Existing but dead. Demidicus has a special relationship with the underworld and with Hades. He told me that dragons go back to the mountain when they die, to a Summerland of light and warmth where peace reigns. They go back to the goddess. He said, because I had Tavyss's tooth, I'll go there too. It's part of me, merged with me. Demidicus could smell it in my blood. He told me the Fates won't have me because I am dragon now." She sighed heavily. "I don't remember that place from when I was dead, but I do remember a light. So, you see, I will be with Tavyss and Phineas again someday."

"Oh, Medea..." Isis said. An unspoken apology hung in the air between them. Rhys thought, when it came to the sisters, words couldn't tell the story that presence and actions did. Isis was here, now, facing what she'd done. By the look on Medea's face, she didn't need anything more.

"I don't regret you bringing me back, sister. I need to be alive." Medea placed a hand on her lower belly, now disturbingly flat. "For our revenge. I must take it since they cannot. I have to believe that."

Rhys stood by while Circe and Isis pulled their sister into a firm hug. Power pulsed in the air when they touched. He'd felt it before, but this time, it was more noticeable. When the hair on his arms and the back of his neck stood on end and a static shock traveled through him, he could not explain it away as a natural phenomenon. He'd seen what the sisters could do. He now recognized their power.

There was witchcraft, and then there were the Three Sisters.

All of them left the ship in a deep and somber silence, the full weight of what they'd lost last night heavy on their shoulders. Hungry, thirsty, and exhausted, he thought his legs might give out by the time they reached the temple in the desert of Niven, but Rhys was confident his friend would not turn him away. He climbed the steps to the stone building and knocked three times. The door opened, and an elf in tan robes greeted them.

"I'm here to see Daluk of Niven," he rasped.

"Rhys Bloodgood." Daluk appeared in his scribe's robes, his smile fading as he perused him and the three sisters. They must have been a sight, filthy and covered in blood from handling Medea's body. Circe's transfiguration had worn off hours ago, and Medea was back in her gown, still stained with dragon blood and the memories of those who were slain while she lay dying. Daluk took one look at her and gave the other scribe a gesture of dismissal. "Thank you, Vuklee. I will handle this."

"We need your help. Something terrible has happened—"

Daluk raised a hand. "Come. You need rest and food, then we will talk."

Circe had never seen an elf in person before they'd arrived in Rogos, and she was fascinated as a slender woman with long, pointed ears led her and her sisters to rooms in the east wing of the temple. The elf was tall and lithe with orange eyes that seemed lit from within, and Circe thought she'd never seen a more magical creature.

"What is this place?" she asked her.

"The Temple of the Sacred Pools. We are an order of scribes who use the goddess's tears to record the history of Ouros in our scrolls."

"The goddess's tears?"

The elf nodded. "The Goddess of the Mountain was once Zeus's lover. When Hera discovered her, she was cast out of the realm of the gods, but Zeus gave her Ouros as her own, a place Hera can never come. It is said that Aitna cried for a century in the beginning. It is her tears that fill our sacred pools."

"I'd never heard the history," Circe said, remembering Hera's jealous rage in the Garden of the Hesperides. It was easy for her to believe every word was true.

"It is my pleasure to host you both and Queen Medea."

Medea's eyebrows rose. "You know who I am?"

"Of course," the scribe said. "We witnessed and recorded everything that happened last night."

Circe met her sister's eyes. "Then you can prove Medea isn't responsible for the massacre!"

The scribe frowned. "I'm afraid that wouldn't be possible."

Medea raged. "How can you say such a thing? How

can you admit you know what happened and not be willing to share it with the rest of Ouros!"

The scribe bowed her head, absorbing Medea's anger with a grace Circe admired. "You are safe here in Rogos, Queen Medea, because our kingdom is and always has been neutral. No other kingdom has power here. None but elves may walk on our soil without our permission. But our neutrality comes at a price. Neither Paragon nor Darnuith will recognize the truth recorded in an elf's scrolls, even if you could get permission from our High Lord for us to share them. Nochtbend and Everfield might in this case, but they have no power to influence Paragon or Darnuith. I am afraid the truth is only useful when there are those who want to hear it and who are in a position to do something about it." She placed a long-fingered hand over her heart. "However, personally, you have my allegiance. I hope, in some small way, I can bring you comfort this day."

It was impossible to rage at someone like this, someone who spoke the truth so calmly, who understood her limitations. Circe glanced at Medea and Isis. There was no fight left in them. Not in any of them. She said nothing to the scribe, just nodded.

Without another word, they were each led to their own rooms. Circe almost cried when she saw the hot bath and fresh clothing waiting for her. She locked the door behind her, locked out the world, then stripped down and slid into the water.

Circe didn't realize she'd fallen asleep in the warm bath until she started to dream. The water lapped her skin. Her eyelids were closed and heavy on her cheeks, but at the same time, she was fully dressed and somewhere else, standing in a hazy darkness.

"Medea?" Circe sensed her sister nearby, although she couldn't see a thing.

"I'm here."

"So am I," Isis said from her other side. "We're dreaming."

"Together, is that possible?" Circe asked.

"It's happening," Isis said. "I can't see either of you, and I can't control the shadows here."

"Come closer. Follow my voice." Circe held out her hands, and soon Isis and Medea stepped from the fog. "This is new."

Medea toyed with the jewel around her neck. The grimoire. "Our powers are growing."

Color flashed in front of her. Circe concentrated as images danced in the fog between them. "Are you seeing this?"

"Yes." Medea's voice sounded breathless. "Isis?"

"I see it." Isis chewed her lip. "It's the future, Medea."

"Alternative futures," Circe said. "See, it's changing." The images kept coming. In each, the three of them attempted to avenge Tavyss. They faced off against Eleanor and Brynhoff in an endless number of ways. And in each of them, they ended up dead. Different scenarios played out, one after the other. They watched themselves die again and again.

"Show me Eleanor's death!" Medea shouted.

The images flashed faster, flashed into the future. Generations passed. The images slowed, became clear. Three sisters, descendants, and a baby, the child of a dragon and witch just like Medea's lost Phineas. Circe cried as she watched them open the golden grimoire and use it to kill Eleanor. The last image was of Eleanor's death. Before their eyes, she turned to dust and her heart was crushed under the heel of a boot.

Circe exchanged glances with her sisters. It was clear they'd seen what she had seen. There was only one scenario that ended in Eleanor's death. The space they were in plunged into darkness.

Circe woke with a start. She was back in her room in the temple. Still in the tub. Only, the water was cold, and her fingers had wrinkled from the long soak.

Water splashed on the floor as she shot up and dried off quickly. The clothing she'd been given was too large for her, but she wasn't going to complain. She cinched the belt and rolled the sleeves. Then she went in search of her sisters. She didn't have to go far. Both of them were in the hallway looking for her.

"Did you—"

"Yes—"

"You too?"

Medea grabbed her hand, and Isis took her other one. They closed the circle, holding on to one another until the buzz of magic built between them. "That wasn't a dream. It was a vision," Isis said.

Medea's face reddened with anger. "No. We don't know that. It could have been a dream."

"We know," Circe said. "When have we ever all

dreamed the same thing? The meaning was clear. If we try to kill Eleanor now, we will fail, and at least one of us will die. Only our descendants, the three sisters who are to come, will be able to kill her."

Isis made a sound deep in her throat. "Do you think it was a vision or a prophecy?"

"Sister?" Circe wasn't sure she understood the difference. Wasn't a vision of the future the same as a prophecy?

"A vision shows us what might be. It's a possibility. A prophecy is a promise. It shows us what will be, if we allow the future to unfold as the Fates intend it."

The fury rolling off Medea sent a shock up Circe's arm. She yelped and tried to yank her hand away.

"I want to kill her. I want to kill her now!" Medea's hands balled into fists and pressed into the sides of her head. Flushed red, she squeezed her eyes shut.

Pain like Circe had never felt before poured into her, coming off her sister in waves. They'd always had a connection. As triplets, she couldn't remember a time they didn't finish one another's thoughts. But this felt as if Medea had turned the trickle between them into a gushing geyser. Emotion jetted into her and stole her breath. She clutched at her chest.

Protective shadows gathered around Isis, and her eyes shifted red. "Stop, Medea. Stop! It's too much!"

"Too much," she spat. "What I'm feeling is too much for you? It's only a fraction of the grief burning in my soul. Tavyss is dead. Phineas is dead. I never even got to hold him in my arms! Either of them!" She pulled Tavyss's heart from her satchel. "This is all I have left of the man who was my world, my life, my very soul!" Her voice cracked, and tears streamed down her face.

"I'm so sorry, Medea." Circe reached for her.

"Don't be sorry. Be angry! Eleanor is immortal. I will die and never get to see her punished."

Isis frowned. "You did see it. Just now, in the future. We need to make sure that future happens. We need to preserve the book for the future sisters, for the ones who will come after us. They'll need it to destroy her."

Medea groaned and started to weep. Tentatively, Circe gathered her into her arms. A cold, dark feeling came over her as she held her sister, and she narrowed her eyes on Isis. "There is one person who should pay, someone who wasn't in our vision."

Medea pressed her hands into her stomach and said the name through her teeth. "Zelaria."

"She is as culpable in all of this as Eleanor."

Isis's shadows swirled with her mounting anger. "We can't go back to Darnuith. By now, she's smeared all our names and has royal guards hunting for us."

The door at the end of the hall opened, and the female scribe they'd met before charged in. "You must come quickly. There's been news."

NINETEEN

Rhys would have ripped off his own skin to save Circe the pain and horror of what she was about to hear. He could barely believe the brazenness of it. Part of him was surprised the evil that had been in their midst had fit within the body of Zelaria. He hated her. Hated her with everything he had in him.

"A friend of the temple sent a falcon this morning with a copy of the *Daily Dragon*, Paragon's most circulated newspaper. I think you need to hear this." Daluk unrolled the scroll and began to read. "Tragedy in the Palace. It is with heavy hearts that we report that last night, the entire Council of Elders, including Queen Eleanor and King Brynhoff's parents, Villania and Falkon, were massacred by the former witch queen of Darnuith, Medea Tanglewood. Medea used her sorcery to capture and enslave Tavyss in her enthrall. She used him to mount an attack upon Paragon, slaughtering dozens of innocent dragons.

"Thanks to the brave and selfless response of King

Brynhoff, the dragon responsible was beheaded. Without her enthralled dragon to protect her, the witch queen likewise fell swiftly under Brynhoff's sword. But that was not the end of the horror.

"A monster tore from the witch's womb, half witch, half dragon. Brynhoff attacked, but the beast was impervious to his blade. It killed a number of guards before succumbing to its injuries. An autopsy by the palace magician confirmed that had the beast been carried to term, it would have been invincible, capable of leveling the mountain.

"As such, King Brynhoff has issued a decree forbidding the mating of dragons and witches. Although the attack by Darnuith was thwarted, and the kingdom's new ruler, Zelaria, promises peace, relations between the kingdoms have never been worse. Witches living in Paragon have had their property seized and been asked to return to Darnuith. Although some trade is still happening along the Sanguine, the future of diplomatic relations between the two kingdoms is anyone's guess.

"The two sisters of Queen Medea are still at large. Queen Eleanor has offered ten thousand dragmar for anyone who can bring them to justice. Rest assured, citizens of Paragon, we are in good hands with Eleanor and Brynhoff on the throne."

Power built in the air like a gathering storm. The three sisters clung to one another. Rhys had never seen Circe look so angry. Medea's skin glowed ominously. And the room filled with the whispers of shadows that twisted and tangled around Isis.

Daluk lowered the scroll. "You are, of course,

welcome to sanctuary in our temple for as long as it takes for you to find a permanent place to settle."

Circe scowled. "A permanent place? Who else would take us in after that? Who could we trust? Ten thousand dragmar? All of Ouros will want our heads!"

Medea folded her arms over her borrowed robes. Her voice was calm and commanding as she said, "We must go back to Darnuith."

Circe gasped. "Are you mad? I understand you wanting to see Tavyss again, but I won't let you commit suicide, Medea. Darnuith would be suicide."

Medea's gaze locked on Rhys's, and a chill traveled through him at what he saw there. "We must find a way, Rhys."

"Why are you looking at him? Keep him out of this. He's a wanted man there as well," Circe protested.

"I'm looking at him because as an apothecary, he knows the woods of Darnuith. He knows every inch of those mountains. Every river. Every stream. Every edible plant."

Rhys nodded. He did know those things. Isis may know her hunting grounds, but Rhys collected herbs and roots from the furthest reaches of the kingdom.

"Why do we need to go back at all, sister?" Isis asked.

Rhys was wondering the same thing. She couldn't be under the delusion that she could wrest the kingdom from Zelaria's grip. The former adviser had too much popular support.

Medea's face was somber as she answered. "We have to retrieve the Tanglewood tree."

Circe's hand went to her mouth. "We grew a new one before."

"It can be used against us. I had it moved to the gardens at Maelhaven. Zelaria knows it is important to me. It's only a matter of time before she discovers why."

Isis cursed.

"What's the Tanglewood tree?" Rhys asked.

Circe looked as if she might be sick as she answered. "Remember how I told you my sisters and I were born in the Garden of the Hesperides? A tree sprouted from the earth in the exact spot of our birth, watered by our blood. Our magic is tied to it. Our wands are made from it."

The pieces came together for Rhys, and he understood why the sisters had to get it back. In the wrong hands, the Tanglewood tree could be analyzed, the magic used to create spells to find and to bind them. If Zelaria understood the tree's magic, she could make slaves of the sisters.

He cracked his neck. "We can cross the border behind Franwise Farm, hike through the gila vine field, then traverse the Ice Forest. It won't be easy, but no one travels that route."

"I can carry us by shadow from the Ice Forest to Maelhaven," Isis said.

Medea nodded. "Daluk, can you procure suitable clothing for our journey?"

"Crafted from the finest elf-made materials."

"Then we leave in the morning," Medea said. Circe and Isis agreed.

"I only have one question," Rhys said. "Once we have this tree, where exactly do you plan to go with it?"

THAT NIGHT, Rhys couldn't sleep. He thought about using some of the herbs from his apothecary's basket to make a sleeping tonic, but since it was already the middle of the night, he was worried he'd be groggy in the morning if he did. He had to be at his best. All of them did, if they had any hope of making it on to palace grounds and retrieving the tree. And that was just the beginning. Then, somehow, they needed to make it somewhere safe.

Where would they go? The Temple of the Sacred Pools wasn't a permanent solution. What would happen to his apothecary? He was sure he loved Circe, but this situation seemed impossible. His mind spun and raged against the changes ahead.

A soft knock came through the darkness. If he'd been asleep, he doubted he'd have heard it. He climbed from his bed and unlocked his door.

"Room enough for two?" Circe asked from the hall.

He pulled her inside and into his arms. "They keep the men separate from the women here. You're breaking the rules." He grinned at her. "I thought you hated to break the rules."

"It's growing on me. Practically becoming a habit."

He cupped her face and kissed her with all the passion he'd had bottled up since the night before. It took everything he had to pull away from her. "As much as I'd love to take you to bed and do more of that, we should actually rest. Big day tomorrow."

"That's what I came to tell you," she said. "We found a place to go."

He guided her to the bed and slid in beside her. "To go... permanently? Where? How?"

"A new world. Daluk saw it in the goddess's tears. He's helping Medea with a few arrangements. We have to leave the golden grimoire here, or Hera will find us. And Medea wanted a grave for Tavyss. Some other things as well." She looked away from him. "I just left them."

"Tell me about this new world."

"There's an island off the coast of Everfield called Aeaea. Daluk says if we sail past the island, we can cross through a portal to another dimension. It's a secret but known to the scribes here from ancient days. There's a world there. A different world from Ouros, where we'll be safe."

Rhys shook his head, his muscles tensing. "What do you mean a different... world?"

Circe placed her hands, palms together, under her cheek. "It's like how we came from the Garden of the Hesperides. That place was not of this world. It does not exist in Ouros, and this place we will go, it's also a different... dimension. Think of rivers running side by side. Each one contains different water. Each flows at a different rate. When I came here, I jumped from one river into another, and if we sail past this island, we will jump into yet another."

Rhys closed his eyes. A different *world*. Could that really be the answer? His heart pounded. He was not a man prone to anxiety, but his palms grew sweaty as he pondered the idea. She may have come from a different world, but Ouros was all he'd ever known. His parents were buried here. June was buried here.

"I don't think I can do it," he said.

"Hmm?"

"I love you, Circe, but I can't go with you."

"Why not?" She sat up and stared down at him from above. "You can't go back to Darnuith. Zelaria knows it was you who broke us out of the dungeon."

"I know. I know I can't go back to Darnuith. I'll petition the High Lord to stay in Rogos, and if that doesn't work, I'll take a position in Everfield. Fairies always need apothecaries. Very few have magic. Have your sisters thought of settling in Everfield?"

Circe shook her head, her stomach tucked as if he'd punched her in the gut. "We can't go to Everfield, Rhys. The goddess showed us in her tears where we must go if we are to survive. My sisters and I..." She toyed with the edge of the blanket. "We see things. We see the future. You have to believe me that this is what we are meant to do."

He swallowed. He loved her. Goddess, he did. But moving to a new *world*... it was insane. It was...unnatural. And if he was being honest, the very idea of it horrified him.

"I... can't," he said honestly. He closed his eyes, unable to watch the disappointment on her face.

She tossed back the covers and stood. "I understand."

"Where are you going?"

"Back to my room."

He reached for her. "This could be the last night we have to spend together."

She smiled sadly at him. "And if that's your choice, then it's best we spend it apart."

TWENTY

The next morning, Circe woke early and dressed in the clothing Daluk had provided for her. She met her sisters in the dining hall for breakfast. Rhys joined them as well, but she carefully kept her eyes on her porridge rather than engage with him. It didn't stop him from trying.

"Circe..." His voice was soft in her ear.

"We should get going," she said. She scooped the last bite of porridge into her mouth and abandoned her empty bowl on the table. She could feel her sisters' eyes on her back as she donned the pack the elves had prepared for her and made her way out the door.

They were taken by carriage to the border, where they started their hike toward Franwise Farm. Soon, they were all ankle deep in the poisonous gila vine. "You're sure this won't hurt us?" Isis asked Rhys.

"If you touch it, don't touch your mouth," he said.

"Noted," Isis replied.

They rounded the farm's protective wards and

descended into the valley of the Ice Forest beyond. Medea pulled the hood of their strange clothing over her ears. "Daluk wasn't kidding about this fabric. It's thin and light but somehow as warm as a fur."

"Mine too," Isis said. "It's as insulating as my hunting parka."

Circe said nothing. She hadn't said a word since they'd left the temple. She was afraid if she parted her lips, all the bitterness she was feeling toward Rhys would fly out of her.

After another hour of walking in silence, Isis stopped abruptly and turned to her. "What in Hades is up with you and Rhys? You haven't said a word to each other since we left Rogos."

"Shh," Circe said. "Quiet down. Have you forgotten the people here want us dead?"

Isis gestured toward the frozen ground and the trees encased in ice and laughed. "There are no people here, Circe. Not even Brody comes this deep into the Ice Forest."

"Why not?"

"Skelna," Isis said.

"Who's Skelna?" Medea asked.

"Possessed tree," Isis murmured, waving a hand dismissively. "Now tell me, what's going on, Rhys."

Rhys cleared his throat. "Well, some say Skelna was a witch whose dark magic backfired and turned her into a monster."

Isis grunted. "I wasn't asking about Skelna, and you know it."

Circe saw something move across the ice ahead. "Whatever she is, I think she's here."

Isis turned and gave a long, low whistle. One of the trees pulled up its own roots and stepped toward them, its bark morphing into a face that made Circe want to turn and run. Despite herself, she stepped closer to Rhys.

Isis pulled off her pack and unwrapped an elderbeast roast. No wonder her pack had seemed heavier than theirs. The thing was huge. The tree opened its mouth, and she chucked the meat into its gaping maw. "Follow me. It's best if we are out of her territory by the time she finishes."

Circe did as she was told, resisting the urge to huddle closer to Rhys and instead sidling up to Medea, who was watching Skelna with an odd fascination.

"She's certainly frightening, isn't she?" Medea said absently. "A fine guardian."

"I'd rather not analyze it," Circe said.

Later, when Rhys and Isis were out of earshot, Medea turned to her and raised an eyebrow. "So, what's happening with you and Rhys?"

Circe gave an exasperated sigh. She wasn't getting out of this. Medea was like a dog with a bone. "He doesn't want to go with us to the new world."

Medea's face fell. "You can hardly blame him. It's risky and terrifying. We'll be somewhere we know no one. We know nothing about the land or its people."

"The problem is, I love him." Tears formed in her eyes, freezing as they dropped so that they pinged like glass on the ice sheet.

Medea slipped her gloved hand into hers. "I'm sorry, sister."

Their gazes met. "Me too."

Isis motioned for them, and they hurried across the ice to her. "This is it. The base of Maelhaven. Are you ready? I'm going to attempt to take us directly into the garden. Remember our plan."

Medea toyed with the diamond at her throat. "How could I forget?"

Circe gripped her hand, and then, before she could object, Rhys slipped his fingers into her other one. Shadows crept in from the mountains, the trees. Isis's wand circled above her head, and then they were flying, blowing toward the palace inside a dark wind.

They landed circling the Tanglewood tree. But something was wrong. A shimmer of purple light surrounded them. A ward. *Fuck.* It was a trap. So much for their plan.

"How nice of you to come," Zelaria said. Circe whirled to find the witch striding into the garden, wand raised. She was flanked by six guards who spread out and surrounded them. "I knew if I waited long enough, you'd come for this damned tree. I never understood what it meant to the three of you, but I knew there was something." She narrowed her eyes as her gaze locked on Medea. "Well, well, well. Isn't this a surprise? You're supposed to be dead."

Circe bristled. Rhys squeezed her hand. He was still holding it. Still comforting her. Why? Why, when he planned to leave her?

"Turns out I'm harder to kill than most," Medea quipped.

"I've never shied away from a challenge." Zelaria raised her wand.

"Before you do, just answer me this, Zelaria," Medea said. She toyed with the gem at her neck. Circe saw it then, a fine line like a needle drawing through the ward in front of her, attached to a silver thread as thin as a spiderweb. While Medea distracted Zelaria, she was using her gift for charms to slowly dismantle the wards around them. But it had to be painstakingly slow or Zelaria would notice. "Why did you do it? What did I ever do to you?"

The older woman scoffed. "What did you do? You stole my birthright! You stole my future. You and that *dragon* used your cursed magic to change the outcome of the Sacred Lots for your own gain. Everyone knows it."

Rhys squeezed Circe's hand again and, with the slightest incline of his head, gestured toward the wards. What did he expect her to do? She was never good at dismantling wards, and Medea was on it anyway.

Then it came to her. Wards. Rhys had mentioned they were commonly designed for people, not animals. She hadn't used that piece of advice to get into Paragon because she needed to keep herself whole to transform him and Isis back. But if he was right... She reached for Isis's hand.

Can you veil Rhys in shadow?

Her sister's eyes flashed red, and darkness gathered around her ankles.

"As much as you may want to believe that I tampered with the Sacred Lots, I didn't," Medea snapped. Her magic finished its side-to-side ascent through the ward, beginning a downward plunge. Her magic needle formed a grid. One pull of that magical string and the ward would shatter. A little more time.

"Everything would have been so simple if you and your spawn had just died when I poisoned you. We could have blamed Paragon, and I could have ruled without further incident. But no, your sister and her apothecary had to go and cure you. That's when I had to get Eleanor involved. Oh, all she wanted was Tavyss dead, and since I wanted you dead, the plan came together nicely. You will go down in history as a monster, and I have taken my place as rightful queen."

The shadows had wrapped around Rhys until he was nothing but a silhouette behind her. She did her best to block him with her body.

"The only monster here is you," Medea said. "You're a murderer."

Circe gripped her wand, still inside her sleeve, and she pointed the tip at Rhys.

"What are you doing there?" Zelaria seethed, finally noticing Isis's shadows. "It won't work. The wards are made to prevent you from traveling, even by shadow."

"*Metamorfóno,*" Circe whispered.

Rhys spiraled and dissolved, leaving behind a pile of his clothing.

"What is this? Where'd he go?" Zelaria yelled. "Guards! Now! Execute them." She twirled her wand but never got a chance to release her spell. Rhys, in the form of a rat, leaped onto her face, dug his claws in, and sank his teeth into her hand. She screamed and dropped her wand, flailing her arms in an attempt to get the massive rat off her.

Medea yanked the string of her charm as more spells flew from the surrounding guards. The ward around them shattered. Glowing brighter than a star, Medea stepped forward, wand raised. The grimoire pulse with power at her throat.

Circe, protect Rhys! Isis screamed down their psychic connection.

Blinded by Medea's light, Circe threw herself in Rhys's direction, her fingers sinking into his fur as Medea's spell began to burn. Shadows drew them both back, wrapped around them, sheltered them.

"Now!" Isis screamed.

Through a cocoon of swirling shadow, Circe watched a pulse of pure celestial power flow out from her sister. Every tree in the garden flattened to the ground, burned to a crisp. Zelaria screamed, her skin blackening as she toppled. The guards did the same. One managed a shield, but it shattered in seconds. He crumpled, leveled to the dirt like everything else. Even Isis's shadows were tearing apart under the force of Medea's will and the power of the book. Circe sheltered Rhys with her body the best she could.

"Medea!" Isis screamed. "Stop! It's done."

Medea turned to face them. Her entire body trembled with power. Her eyes were entirely black and glowing with strange otherworldly energy. Was she even in there anymore?

"Medea, please!" Isis begged as another of her

shadows turned to ash. "Circe, help. I don't think she can hear me."

Circe raised her wand and pointed it at her sister, Isis's shadow's parting for her. "*Metamorfóno!*" she screamed, panting with the effort as the spell locked on Medea and warred with the deadly fire she was putting off. Tongues of purple lashed at her, but Circe hung on.

At last, Medea twirled in her robes and disappeared. A narwit crawled from the elfin fabric, wiggling its ears. Medea's deadly magic settled like shattered stars around them, its twinkling residue sinking harmlessly into the scorched earth.

Isis dropped her shadow shield, openly weeping by Circe's side. She was spent. It had taken all of Isis's power to hold off Medea's magic. When Medea had unleashed the book in anger, she'd unleashed something dark within herself. Something ancient and feral. A few seconds more and it would have torn them both to shreds.

Slowly Circe stood. She was exhausted, but she dug deep and, with a flick of her wrist, sent a spell into the rat she'd shielded with her body. Rhys transformed back into a man. He surveyed the devastation around him and hobbled toward his clothes.

She was about to bring Medea back when movement to her left caught her eye. She limped over to a charred figure writhing at the edge of the scorched earth. By some miracle or magic, Zelaria was still alive.

Circe hovered over her, anger bolstering her power. Zelaria's skin was black, and she was bleeding in places, but her eyes followed Circe. She was still in there.

"Isn't this a surprise? You're supposed to be dead." Circe echoed the words the witch had said to her sister. She scoffed. "I've never shied away from a challenge. *Metamorfóno.*"

The once-powerful Zelaria transformed into a dung beetle. Rhys arrived at her side, looked at the beetle, then at Circe.

"No rule against killing a bug," he said.

She raised her boot and ground Zelaria under her heel.

RHYS WAS A HEALER. He was a man who'd devoted his life to ending people's suffering. From childhood, he'd hated to watch anything die. But despite all that, he couldn't bring himself to feel the least bit of remorse for Zelaria.

He felt nothing but relief as Circe wiped her remains from the bottom of her boot and directed a spell toward the narwit that was once her sister. Medea appeared in a squat where the small pink animal had just stood. Rhys thanked the Fates that her eyes had returned to normal again and that the horrific celestial fire she'd been putting off was contained again. Isis ran to her and helped her dress.

"Circe," he whispered.

She turned to him, exhausted now. She tucked her wand away as if she couldn't bear the weight of it in her hand any longer. She tucked a few stray strands of her dark hair behind her ears before she spoke. "I've been thinking, Rhys. With Zelaria and the royal guards dead, it might be safe for you to return to your apothecary. You can get Daluk to vouch for you that you were in Rogos the entire time. Deny your involvement in our escape. There's likely no hard proof against you, and with us gone, they'll welcome you back with open arms. The people of Darnuith always loved you. They'll come around once we've left."

"I'd like to go home," he said. "The only problem is, I don't think my home is in Mistcraven anymore."

She sighed. "I'm sure Everfield would take you in. Anyone would."

"It's funny how having one's life flash before their eyes will change a person." Rhys had looked out through those wards at Zelaria and the deadly magic that surrounded them, and only one thing had crossed his mind. "When I thought I would die today, all I could think of was how content I was to die with you."

She frowned and shook her head. "Rhys..."

"I have loved you, Circe, in a way I never imagined my heart could again. And the thought of being apart from you feels more like death than what happened just moments ago."

She wiped a hand over her face. "I'm too tired for this. What are you trying to say?"

He grabbed her by the shoulders. "I'm saying that you are surely a master of transfiguration because you've transformed this heart. I am not the same. I never will be. And I can't go home because home is right here with you. Wherever you go. Wherever you are. That's home to me now."

Her eyes widened. "You're coming with us to the new world?"

He nodded. "I am. On one condition."

"What's that?"

"Marry me, Circe. In this world, or the next. Bind yourself to me."

She wrapped her arms around him, her body leaning into his strength. "I think I'd better say yes. It would be hard living the rest of my life without my heart. It's yours, you know. Always has been."

He cradled the base of her skull and sealed the promise with a kiss. Only when she started to laugh did he pull back. "What's so funny?"

She raised her wand, and a rat's whisker he hadn't noticed before retracted into his cheek. "Missed one," she said.

He wiped a hand across his smile and met her lips again.

EPILOGUE

The ship that Circe found herself on several weeks later was nothing like the ships of Ouros. It was made entirely of wood and metal with no magic to hold it together. A cloth sail caught the wind over her head and propelled the ship forward. It pitched from side to side with every monstrous wave in this strange, tumultuous sea.

They'd traveled from Everfield around the island of Aeaea to a place called Crete, where they boarded a ship to Provence, France using gold they'd taken from the palace. Gold, it seemed, was as valuable in this world as in Ouros.

They were able to use spells and enchantments to bridge the language barrier but had to be careful to hide what they were doing. The people here were without magic. Even the smallest spell seemed to scare them and send them off crossing themselves.

They used the money they had on hand to procure a small residence above a store. They'd thought to make it into an apothecary until they'd learned that bread sold better than any tonic in the marketplace. Within days, they'd set up a bakery and infused their bread with herbs that Rhys collected from the countryside. The resulting loaves were so delicious, anyone who tried one came back for more.

Dressed in a gown purchased with their newfound wealth, Circe married Rhys in a small ceremony in a chapel in rural Provence with her sisters by her side. It was a beautiful ritual, although strange. This new world had different gods and peculiar customs. In Darnuith, it was common for the man to take the woman's surname when they married. Here, it was suggested that Circe would take the name of Bloodgood. It took only a slight manipulation of the parchment to change Rhys's last name to Tanglewood. And so, the name Bloodgood was left at the altar, and the four of them lived happily in Provence for many years.

One day, illness came to Provence, something the townspeople called the plague. There were whispers. Circe learned that, in other areas of this world, those thought to be witches were burned at the stake for spreading the boils that killed the humans.

Rhys was able to create a tonic to cure the infection, but no one in Provence would take it. Speculation rose. Isis was called a spawn of the *devil*. The sisters and Rhys didn't know this devil but assumed he must be similar to the god Hades. When the local seamstress accused Medea of being a witch, the human woman ran screaming when Medea didn't deny it. After that, Rhys and Circe heard rumors that the neighbors would be coming with pitchforks to drag them to the stake for burning.

It was hard moving again, but Isis had heard talk of a place called *La Nouvelle-Orléans,* a new land where few people had settled before. Her shadows carried them to the port, where they used their wealth to buy passage to this new land.

"What do we know about this place?" Rhys asked. He positioned the Tanglewood tree in its pot next to the bed in their stateroom. They'd used spells to shrink it down and make it more manageable. The tree's shiny green leaves gave off their own light in the dim interior.

Medea sighed. "Isn't it enough that it is far away from where they burn witches who are not even witches? I am told there are fewer of these humans there and plenty of land on which to build a home. I thought we might return to farming."

Isis took a seat in what looked to be a very uncomfortable chair. "Can't be any worse than baking bread all day."

"I rather enjoyed baking bread." Circe shrugged. "But a new place might mean new herbs. Perhaps we could open an apothecary in this new land."

Rhys winked at her. "With a little magic, it should be easy enough to establish ourselves. Despite the human obsession with witches, we seem to be the only four in this world."

Circe grinned at him and then at her sisters. She'd been keeping a secret, wanting to give Medea time to heal. But it was a secret that couldn't be kept any longer. "Five."

No one moved. It was as if her sisters and Rhys were holding their breath. She ran a hand protectively over her abdomen.

"Sister?" Isis asked.

"I'm pregnant," Circe confirmed. She beamed up at the family she loved, praying for their acceptance.

"Blessed Fates," Rhys murmured, pulling her into his arms. He couldn't hold back his joy. He kissed her and then the small mound of her belly.

Circe looked toward Medea and Isis. "I am almost certain it's a girl."

"Maybe two," Isis said softly.

"Maybe three," Medea added. Circe saw a flicker of hope in her eyes. Hope for the future they'd seen in their vision. Three sisters who'd take their revenge on Eleanor. They exchanged knowing smiles.

Rhys cleared his throat beside her. "Or just one. Honestly, one more Tanglewood might be all this world can handle."

She smiled at him and her sisters. Her love. Her life. After all the places she'd been, she knew for sure that family was the only thing that mattered, and love, in all its forms, was far more important than geography. She kissed Rhys lightly on the cheek. "Maybe... For now."

THANK you for reading **TANGLEWOOD MAGIC!** If you enjoyed this title, please leave a review wherever you buy books.

The three sisters are on their way to New Orleans to

start a new life. But Isis is dealing with demons—both the personal kind and those that dwell in the underworld. When a chance at love comes along, she'll have to face the darkness, or risk losing everything. Read Isis's story in TANGLEWOOD LEGACY, available now.

AVAILABLE NOW
TURN THE PAGE TO READ AN EXCERPT

EXCERPT: TANGLEWOOD LEGACY

Isis Tanglewood jackknifed off the bed as two glowing red eyes faded from her memory. The nightmare again. She held her head, wiping tears she couldn't remember shedding from under her eyes. She'd been crying in her sleep again. Ever since she'd raised Medea from the dead, she'd suffered dreams that left her heart pounding and her breath short. Dreams that were more than dreams if she was honest with herself. The worst part was, she couldn't even seek out the comfort of her sisters. How could she tell Medea that when she'd descended into Hades to resurrect her, accidentally leaving her unborn son behind, that something else, something *evil*, had taken notice of her and now haunted her at night?

She had enough trouble looking Medea in the eye. Could she ever forgive herself for that terrible mistake? Phineas. Oh goddess, she'd planned to name the boy Phineas.

Throwing back the covers, she leaped from her bed

and rushed to the chamber pot. Her heart beat a mad tattoo within her chest, her stomach somersaulting in the wavering room. Wait, that wasn't in her head. Isis remembered she was on a ship bound for *La Nouvelle-Orléans,* or as the English called it, New Orleans. The sickness she was feeling wasn't from her nightmares at all, but from the roiling of the wooden vessel on the mighty sea.

She grabbed her robe and slipped it on over her nightgown, then flung open the door to her quarters and headed for the upper deck. She needed air. Needed to see the stars, feel the comforting witness of the moon, and connect with the magic that night breathed into her.

Shadows gathered around her ankles. The darkness was trying to comfort her as it always did when she was anxious. Only, for the first time in her life, their presence wasn't entirely welcome. The darkness in her nightmare —the demon with the red eyes—also commanded shadows, and with the memory of his presence fresh in her mind, the tendrils that snaked around her calves felt too much like his touch.

As her bare feet fell on the wooden deck and the warm sea air blew back her dark hair, Isis tried to put the demon out of her mind. The dream was always the same. He wanted her. Wanted to be with her. And the worst part was, as horrifying a visage as the demon possessed, the dream filled her with lust as certainly as it filled her with fear. This particular demon knew how to turn on the charm.

She looked out over the railing toward the singular moon, so different from the night sky of Ouros, and wondered if there was a spell to protect her from her own mind. Her own guilt.

"You too? Bad dreams?" A woman's voice came from behind her, and Isis whirled. She understood the woman's French clearly enough, but her accent was different from what she'd picked up in Provence. *Paris*, she guessed. The woman had the dark curly hair and gray eyes of many she'd met from that region.

"Yes. Is it obvious?" Isis asked.

The woman pulled her robe tighter around her slight frame. She was too thin and too pale, hair dull. Isis had seen it before in other travelers. The sickness took hold, extinguishing the spark in their eyes before slowly draining them of life. "I only assumed as that is why I came up. I think it's the sea. The roiling of the boat does something to my mind. I've never slept well, not one night since we've been on this bloody boat." She arched an eyebrow. "I'm Delphine, by the way. Delphine Devereaux."

"*Enchante*, Delphine. How is it we haven't met before? Have you been in Haiti long?"

"Only long enough to switch vessels. Our original ship is returning to France," Delphine said.

When Isis had set off from Provence with her sisters and Rhys, they'd intended to travel straight to America, but a storm had blown their ship off course, and they'd initially ended up in Haiti. They'd stayed for several months, until once again, their subtle use of magic started to call attention to them. They took no precautions but were never ill. They had no servants, yet their home was always well tended. Food appeared on their table although they employed no cook. Eventually people started to notice, and the whispers became more heated.

Suspicion alone, though, wasn't enough to drive them on. It was the baby. Circe's pregnancy had advanced. Among their kind, babies were notorious for unexpected magic. They needed a place far away from the bustling crowd, a place where they could be safe from human interference.

"You didn't mention your name," Delphine said, shaking her from her thoughts.

"Oh, excuse me. I'm Isis Tanglewood." She gave the woman a shallow curtsy.

"What an unusual name for a French woman," Delphine said. "You are French, are you not?"

"From Provence." Isis shifted uncomfortably. The secret to a good lie was a partial truth. "My mother heard the name while traveling."

Delphine studied her. "And your destination is la Nouvelle-Orléans?" She scoffed, scanning Isis from head to toe. "Did they find you in a brothel or a convent? With skin like yours, I assume a convent."

Isis attempted to tamp down her offense. She was aware that most of the women on this ship were, in fact, taken from brothels, convents, and prisons and offered new lives as wives to hardened colonists of the territory of Louisiana. This Delphine meant no harm in her inquiry. While men might have many reasons for traveling to the Americas, the women here did not share the social freedoms she'd enjoyed in Darnuith before they'd fled her home world. Still, she couldn't bring herself to lie about this.

"Neither," she said honestly. "My sisters and I wanted to settle somewhere new." When Delphine gave her a strange look, she added. "We travel with my sister's husband, Rhys."

Delphine's mouth opened, and she nodded her understanding. A man explained everything. Isis had to keep herself from rolling her eyes. The culture in this dimension was strange indeed.

"I too travel with my sisters, Lucienne and Antoinette," Delphine said, smiling bitterly. "No husbands, though. I am told we will stay in a convent under the watch of the Ursuline nuns until a suitable match can be made for us. By suitable match, I presume they mean the highest bidder. Whoever is willing to pay for a wife to cook, clean, and warm their bed. After living in the wilds these years, I bet it's the bed-warming they're most in need of, or they wouldn't have sought us out."

Isis frowned. Three sisters, just like them, sold like chattel. The thought upset her, but this was how this realm worked, and there was nothing she could do about the women's fate. "I wish you the best possible outcome."

Delphine opened her mouth to speak but was silenced by a fit of coughing, her face growing paler with her breathlessness until it rivaled the glow of the moon. When she finally stopped, her bottom lip was stained bright red from fresh blood.

The woman was dying. Isis recognized the signs of

the illness the people here called consumption. Rhys had the herbs and magic to cure it, but asking him to do so was out of the question. They'd left Provence and then Saint-Domingue to escape scrutiny. What would be the point if they made the same mistakes here and garnered more accusations of witchcraft?

Still, her heart grew heavy, thinking of the woman's plight. By the way she spoke so freely of warming a man's bed, Isis did not doubt that she likely came from a brothel. She feared Delphine's life had been hard and was about to get harder.

Delphine examined her in the moonlight, coughing again into her hand. Her eyes narrowed. "How is it that after weeks of travel, your skin still glows as if it's lit from within? Your figure hasn't suffered a bit from the gruel they serve us. Your hair shines like a raven's wing."

Isis thought quickly. It would not benefit her or her sisters for their relative health to be questioned. "My sisters and I spent several months with friends on a plantation in Saint-Domingue, regaining our strength after the long journey from France." Isis raised her chin.

"Ah." She scoffed, and Isis saw her eyes turn hard. "A proper lady with friends in high places. Perhaps I shouldn't be speaking so openly above my class." The harsh sting of her tone told her that Delphine didn't think highly of proper ladies.

"I'm quite certain a proper lady wouldn't be on a ship to the wilds of America." Isis heaved a beleaguered sigh. "I hope we can be friends once you've made your new home, Delphine."

The sickly woman made a guttural sound. "Of

course. Now, if you'll excuse me, I find I've grown tired again. Sleep well, Isis." She gave a shallow curtsy and headed for the stairs.

"Delphine?" Isis called, suddenly curious at the talk of sleep. The woman paused her descent and looked at her expectantly. "What was *your* nightmare about?"

The woman smiled a mouth of yellowing teeth. "I dreamed of a red-eyed demon," she said, then grinned wider. "I just hope it wasn't my future husband."

Isis hugged herself against an unexpected chill as Delphine disappeared below deck.

MEET GENEVIEVE JACK

USA Today bestselling and multi-award winning author Genevieve Jack writes wild, witty, and wicked-hot paranormal romance and romantic fantasy. She believes there's magic in every breath we take and probably something supernatural living in most dark basements. You can summon her with coffee, wine, and books, but she sticks around for dogs and chocolate. Her novels feature badass heroines, fiercely loyal heroes, and fantasy elements that will fill you with wonder. Learn more at GenevieveJack.com.

Do you know Jack? Keep in touch to stay in the know about new releases, sales, and giveaways.

Join my VIP reader group
Sign up for my newsletter

facebook.com/AuthorGenevieveJack
twitter.com/genevieve_jack
instagram.com/authorgenevievejack
bookbub.com/authors/genevieve-jack

MORE FROM GENEVIEVE JACK!

The Three Sisters

(Prequel to the Treasure of Paragon)

The Tanglewood Witches

Tanglewood Magic

Tanglewood Legacy

The Treasure of Paragon

The Dragon of New Orleans, Book 1

Windy City Dragon, Book 2,

Manhattan Dragon, Book 3

The Dragon of Sedona, Book 4

The Dragon of Cecil Court, Book 5

Highland Dragon, Book 6

Hidden Dragon, Book 7

The Dragons of Paragon, Book 8

The Last Dragon, Book 9

His Dark Charms

Lucky Me

Lucky Break

Lucky Stars

Knight Games

The Ghost and The Graveyard, Book 1

Kick the Candle, Book 2

Queen of the Hill, Book 3

Mother May I, Book 4

Fireborn Wolves

(Knight World Novels)

Logan (Prequel)

Vice, Book 1

Virtue, Book 2

Vengeance, Book 3

www.ingramcontent.com/pod-product-compliance
Lightning Source LLC
Chambersburg PA
CBHW011927050726
47591CB00009B/2382